The Bond

we share

H.L JONES

THE BOND WE SHARE

THE BOND WE SHARE

H.L JONES

Other titles by author

The bond series
The bond, book one.
The bond we share, book Two.

Disclaimer: contains mature material that might cause triggers

All characters, places, creatures, and events in this book are fictitious and figments of the author's imagination.

Hljonesauthor@hotmail.com
Editor: Brittany Lewis
Editor: Natalie Thompson
Beta readers: Emma Powell, Natalie wood, Mitchell Doohan, Brittany Willetts, and Chantelle Pickering
Cover designer: @ H.L Jones

First Printing, 2021

I am truly blessed to have amazing parents and siblings that love and support me to do and be all I can be and friends that are the incredible forever family friends that share in our successes and help each other through our failures. This book is dedicated to them.

Contents

I

Light In The Dark

It is so quiet. I open my eyes, but it doesn't help me. All I see is darkness. My heart is aching, raw from the loss of my father and Logan. I feel my tears run down my face. I move to wipe them away, but it's so dark that I can't even see my hand in front of me.

The darkness is so thick it feels like it will choke me if I let it in. I had nothing, not even my memories. Then I had Mia and a family, then I lost them and found a new family, now I've lost them too. Is this all my life will ever consist of? Lose and betrayal? My heart sinks further and the darkness gets thicker, it is getting harder to breathe now.

My thoughts go to my father and the emotional rollercoaster ride with him. I enjoyed being around him but when I found out he was my father and not Aiden's, it hurt to think of all the things he had done to keep me from being tainted, but in the end, he gave his life to save me from my uncle and showed me how much he loved me.

The darkness has begun to ease up and I find breathing a little easier now. I move slowly, trying to see if there is anything around me but the space is completely empty. A small light appears and moves towards me. The light is so small, but in the darkness, it can be seen so brightly.

I shake my head. *Why didn't I think of it sooner?* In a flash of dazzling light my deerling bursts to life, lighting up the darkness. "Wow! I didn't expect you to be so big." I bend down slightly. "You're as big as a bear!"

"I am as you need me to be right now." my deerling says. My mouth falls open as I try to process this.

"I have been by your side your whole life. You gave me life. You taught me to love and how to give it to another." He nestles up to my hand that dangles at my side. "I was with you when you were a child. I watched you grow. I was there when Aiden sent you to the other side. I was with you when the most beautiful 18-year-old girl found you."

"Tom?"

"Yes, Bree."

"But I don't understand! How are you my deerling when you're supposed to be with Mia and the kids?"

"Once I was through the portal and in a world with no magic, I was given a physical body. When I saw Mia, I scattered, hiding from her. I didn't know what was going on, but I was always by your side and stayed close. After Mia caught me a few times, she invited me to spend time with you both and that made keeping an eye on you easier over the years. But what I didn't expect was to fall so in love with her. I began to lose track of time and my task. When Mia said we should get married I was so happy and then Mira came along seven years later. I had no idea I could even give her children. I was lost in so much joy. All I could think of was that I wanted her to call our first child 'that was the spitting image of her mother with her auburn hair and hazel eyes,' was

Mini Mia, but she wouldn't have any of it. So, she compromised with me and named her Mira." he chuckles, lost in the memory. "When Chris came along eighteen months later, my own little mini me, I looked into those grey eyes and I was gone. I had fallen so far into my happy place that the day the Akuma attacked I was shocked to my very core. It had stopped occurring to me that today might be the day. I grabbed Mira and Chris, trying to get them to safety and pull Mia with me, but she wouldn't leave you. That's when I realized how far I had strayed from my path, I was torn between my mission and my heart. After you disappeared, Mia was a mess and everything fell apart. I was so torn up that I failed you. I started failing Mia and the kids, too, but as you got stronger, I felt your powers calling to the bond we share. I was given the task to lead you through to your destiny. Many have tried before but failed." explains Tom.

"Failed what?" I interject.

"All will be explained as you progress. No one has ever made it out of the darkness, once they let it in, it overtakes them, completely consuming them." Tom says in a grave tone.

I blink a few times and realize the darkness is part of my test. "That's why I felt like it was choking me." I ask.

"When you were lonely and thinking of all the bad memories you were dying, but when you remembered how you felt loved, it pushed back the darkness. It is still all around us, but you have it in control now."

A giggle escapes me, making Tom raise an eyebrow at my reaction.

"I am so sorry Tom, it's really hard to have a serious conversation with you when you look like a deerling."

Tom chuckles realizing what has me reacting this way. "You can choose my form Bree. I have no physical form here. I'm pure magic. My body is back home with Mia but when you need me your deerling is the best I can use."

"But what happens to your body back home?" I ask as I focus on Tom and what he usually looks like. I listen to him as his form changes to that of the handsome, ash blond haired, grey eyed man I know so well.

"It's like I'm in a deep sleep. Since you last saw Mia, she was feeling like she was going insane. It got so bad that she was going to doctors and psychiatrists to get help. I was doing better now that I was back on track to help you learn your magic, and you seemed to need me less and less. It made things easier for me and I could focus on Mia. That's when I told her the truth. I told her everything. When my body went into my first few sleeps, no one could wake me. The doctors had a hard time figuring it out so I had no choice but to tell Mia everything. She took it far better than I thought she would, actually. Your visit with her made everything so much easier for her to believe, and now she looks forward to me telling her how you're doing and what you get up to."

I shrink a little. "You haven't told her everything, have you?" I ask sheepishly.

Tom smiles at me brightly. "I don't tell her things that will get me killed, if she knew even one percent of what you get up to while under my watch, I would not have to worry about divorce." A wide grin spreads across his face as he winks at me.

I laugh so hard I feel my sides threaten to split. "I missed this so much."

"Me too. Here we have more than enough magic to talk now. Before

I could not do much other than observe, help you with your magic, and try to make you smile when I could."

"Wait a minute, I always thought you were a year older than Mia, if you are of magic what...."

Tom rolls his eyes with a smile cutting me off. "When I met Mia, I said I was one year older than her because that was what I had understood the requirements of a male to be. I had to adapt quickly and learn all I could. One of the perks of being made of pure magic, you are a fast learner and pretty impressive." Tom winks at me boastfully, buffing his nails on his shirt.

I push him as I laugh off his terrible attempt to boast, as Tom is a very humble man it does not work at all for him.

"On a more serious note, that night I tried to go home, I saw there was distance between you both," I say softly.

Tom places his hand under my chin to raise my face to look up at him. "I promise you that was a very dark time for us, but once again you brought us back together Bree. We are stronger than ever now. I have no secrets from her and she can believe in the impossible."

I smile a big smile as my heart fills more and another worry falls from my mind. The room vibrates under our feet as flames shoot up around us, piercing the darkness further. The flames box us in like a giant cage.

"Oh, no! What did I do?" I shriek.

"No, Bree! Don't think negatively. You're doing it!"

"We are in a fire cage! What is progress about this?" I snap.

He laughs, wrapping his arms around me and lifting me off my feet awkwardly. I push at Tom as he lets me back down.

"Progress is knowing Aiden and my friends are okay."

In an instant the fire burns hotter and brighter. The fire twists into a viewing window. I see Aiden and the others still on the platform. I reach out to touch Aiden, but retract my hand quickly as the fire burns me. Aiden turns to me and I swear his deep blue eyes are looking right at me.

2

The World Without Her (Aiden)

"Bree?" The words are out of my mouth before I realize it.

Roxy looks up at me. She is still on the ground. It is so hard to comfort her when all I want to do is scream myself, not to mention I am useless when it comes to emotional outbursts.

One of the reasons I like Roxy is because she is strong and does not let her emotions get the better of her, so in moments like this I feel utterly useless. It has been hard on all of us, not to mention Roxy is too strong to admit she is in love with Metikye, and he is currently comforting a completely distraught Madeline.

I know Bree would know how to handle situations like this, it is at times like this I realize how much I really depend on her.

Her tears stop, and hope shines in her blue eyes, "Why did you call Bree's name just now?" Roxy asks me.

Just thinking of Bree calms me. Maybe she is what we all need right now.

"I know it sounds strange, but I swear I felt Bree reaching out to me." I shake my head listening to my thoughts out loud. "Sounds ridiculous I know, but I felt it."

"Knowing the bond, you and Bree have, it does not sound so far-fetched actually."

Metikye finally makes his way to Roxy, helping her to her feet. The way she looks at him gives her away so easily but Metikye's heart is rivaled by the man's cluelessness. I sigh.

When Madeline sees Roxy she runs over, wrapping her arms around Roxy, giving her a big hug. Although Roxy looks awkward with this show of affection, she does not push her away.

It seems the mere mention of Bree does the trick, giving them hope knowing she is still alive. It drives me mad that so many people seem to need her. All I can think is that she is mine and I need her more. I know I should not feel that way, but I cannot help how I feel.

"We can't do anything if we are all giant messes. I know Bree is okay and I know she is going to need us to be at our best."

Everyone nods and agrees.

"You all heard the maiden speak. This prophecy was never what any of us thought it was, and if Bree felt the need to go, she had good reason. Bree's heart is the purest I have ever known. I cannot believe anything involving her could be bad. She would never allow it and Bree has put her life on the line for that belief." I say firmly.

"How can you be so sure Bree is okay?" one person from the crowd asks, a bustle of voices rumble in agreeance.

"I know she is okay. I feel it in my heart." I reply.

"We can't base our faith and our lives on your feelings, we need more!" another voice shoots back.

"YEAH!" the crowd roars.

"How about me?"

The crowd parts as my mother walks through the crowd. Everyone is quiet as she walks to me, turns, and sits at my side.

"I am Queen Reina."

"For all those who don't understand her, this is my mother Queen Reina." I say in my best authoritative voice I can muster.

Gasps ring out as whispers and chatter erupt.

"QUIET!" I thunder. The space falls silent as I continue to repeat my mother's words to the crowd. "How I came to be this way is irrelevant right now. What matters at this moment is that even though Bree is not with us, I know she is alive because anyone not of light magic sees me in the form of a Bupper puppy. Bree placed this illusion on me to stop people from being afraid and helping me to move around more freely from judgment. If Bree was dead, you would not be able to see this, you would see the Akuma I was cursed to walk as."

A light magic wielder steps forward and confirms my mother's words to be true, while other light magic wielders join her.

"We have lost our king, and our princess is being judged in the maiden, who will lead us through the trials ahead as I am sure none of us are prepared for the darkness that will soon be upon us." an older man yells out.

The crowd nods and agrees as mumbling chatter continues.

"Most of you have been misled with lies as only a small number of us were trusted enough with the truth."

"Who are you to speak of truth?" I ask the young woman harshly.

"I am Larna. You are Bree's dog, I see." she sneers.

"You would be wise to bite that venomous tongue." Madeline hisses, not giving me a chance to bite back.

I run my hand through my shaggy black hair as my temper is rapidly rising.

"Oh, look, another dog from her pack. Bree is nothing more than a lie. The true daughter to the late queen was exiled and replaced by that imposter!" she seethes at Madeline as everyone gasps.

"What possible proof could you have of these outrageous claims?" I ask desperately reining in my temper.

"Not only does Bree look nothing like queen Kate, but I know the people who raised queen Kate's child, because the king chose Bree!"

"Are you implying Bree is no daughter of kintarbie or she has a half-sister?"

"I am saying nothing more than she is no daughter of Queen Kate! Her bloodline to the king is possible if she was a bastard child."

My eyes grow wide at the disgusting way this wretched woman is speaking about Bree, but to my horror, I hear the chatter from the crowd.

"It is no secret the king and queen never showed love for one another." I hear a voice in the crowd yell out.

"How is that any proof?" an on-looker replies.

"Many royal families don't bond for love; they have a duty to their people over their hearts!" someone else retorts.

"Yeah!" the crowd booms.

Larna cuts over the chatter. "So then, the real question here is, was Bree chosen for the people or for the king's heart?"

The entire place erupts, and I see so many turning on Bree and her lineage. I lower my eyes to the ground in disgust, not wanting to make eye contact with any that would think this way of Bree. I clench my fists at my side, my temper seething long past the capacity to control it now.

"You are spiteful and selfish! You know nothing of Bree, or you would not speak of her in such a way. She gave up everything to write someone else's wrong to save us all. She could have let you all suffer and run away with me and never look back, but she chose to save us all and this is how you repay her! YOU DON'T DESERVE HER!" I seethe, my body so overrun with fury that I am shaking.

Luc rests his hand on my shoulder as Metikye, Roxy, Nathaniel and Mac step up to stand at my side.

Madeline moves her face closer to Larna's. "If this real princess of yours is so special, why is she not in the maiden being judged instead of Bree? To me, the real princess was chosen, and she was chosen for no other reason other than the size and power of her heart."

"We don't give a damn what you think!" Nathaniel snaps. His green eyes lighting up in fury.

"She is and will always be *our* princess!" Mac follows running his fingers down his short, trimmed beard.

"Our friend!" Roxy booms with pride.

"And our family!" Metikye finishes, gently bringing the hostility back down.

Larna is still locked in a heated stare down with Madeline. Larna sighs. "None of us can help her where she is now. Bree is on her own. All we can do is keep the lands and its people safe."

"Safe from what?" I ask over the erupting chatter.

"Your Bree is being judged right now, while you can feel her and see Queen Reina's illusion is still in place. We know she has not failed us yet."

Her emphasis on *yet*, makes my fists clench and my mouth twitch.

"But if she succeeds, things will change and panic will wash over the lands."

"What do you mean by change?" More than one person ask's at once.

She flicks her long golden hair over her shoulder. It shimmers a strange barely visible rainbow. I do not think anyone else notices, I think nothing more of it until I see the same rainbow shimmer in her brown eyes.

"The answers we seek are far before our time, but from my understanding, our lands are not as they are supposed to be, and Bree has been chosen to right a wrong done many lifetimes ago."

This conversation is making me very unsettled. Bree suddenly has a possible little sister no one knew about; and she is righting a wrong from many years ago? Something does not sit right with me, but I cannot disregard anything at this moment in time.

"We all need to return to our homelands and warn the people of what is happening. We don't know what will happen and we need to be prepared for any outcome." I say taking back control of the conversation.

"A team of us will stay here and observe the maiden, while the rest of us warn and make preparations. I know you all still have questions, we all do, but right here and right now this is the best course of action we can take."

A loud rumble shakes the platform, making everyone drop to the floor bracing themselves. After a few moments it slowly subsides. The waterfalls around the edge rapidly stops and dries up. A crack sounds above and everyone looks to the gate to Aquilla. Everyone gasps, and fear erupts.

The gateway to Aquilla now has a small crack and is slowly dripping water onto the maiden platform. I call the Oregrin's to the docking station, to start loading people onto them. One by one they descend.

"Everyone on!" I boom over the loud crowd. They are too afraid to refuse my orders.

Things get out of hand as people push and pull trying to be the ones to depart first. Metikye steps forward to get some control back and for a moment everyone quietens, waiting for Metikye's move. When nothing comes, everyone starts to talk again. Metikye looks at me with confusion and..... is that fear?

The crowd seems to think the same. One by one they try desperately to use their magic, but nothing happens. One by one they all look to the other in the hope that someone will show some sign of magic, but it seems Logan was not the only one. It is only fitting, that there would be no magic in a world without her.

3

⸎

A Time Long Forgotten

The blaze burns hotter and the flames around me erupt, changing my view of Aiden. It takes everything I have to fight the heat of the flames and look through to the scene I see before me while I nurse the burns to my hand. Beautiful colors of blue and purple dance through the flames drawing me in.

"Leandra? Leandra? Where are you?" A handsome man in purple robes calls. A giggle sounds behind a tree as a beautiful garden comes into focus. "Leandra." he smiles.

"I thought you were not coming."

"I could never stay away if you called for me Mitace." His smile widens further, showing off his perfectly white teeth.

"With all the preparation for tonight's festival viewing I thought for sure you would not have the time."

"As I said before, I will gladly make the time. Now whatever possessed you to call for me at such a busy time?"

"Come with me." Mitace says with excitement. He grabs her arm and pulls her from behind the tree where she was hiding. She laughs joyfully as Mitace runs with her hand in his through the trees until a magnificent temple comes into view.

"Why did you want to come here?" she asks him.

"This is the first place that we met. Don't you remember?" he asks, pulling some stray leaves that have caught in her long golden hair.

"Yes, of course I remember. You had fallen from a tree collecting fruit, you came here and that is when I saw you, I cleaned your wounds while we talked that's when we first became friends. Not much has changed, you are still just as clumsy as ever." she giggles.

"That was one hundred years ago today. I simply thought it was worth celebrating."

"I truly don't understand the sentiment but if you feel so deeply about it, how shall we celebrate?" she asks.

"The viewing tonight, let us go together."

"Very well, if that is your wish. We can meet up later tonight and watch the festivities together." she smiles. He takes her hand and presses a kiss to the back of her hand. Her smile falters for a moment. "What did you just do?" she asks.

"The dwellers below do it as a sign of respect, I believe. I just thought it fitting."

Her smile returns. "I have never known anyone to be so knowledgeable of the underlings, time for us is unlike time for them and their ways are damming. Please be careful not to fall too deep in getting to know them. I would hate to see you break any of the rules, they are there to keep balance."

Mitace smiles a half-smile. "Yes, of course. I just thought it was a sweet gesture you deserved."

"The gesture is received in good grace. I must go. I'll see you again later tonight." she beams as she leaves, while Mitace looks on longingly after her.

The fire burns and I lose focus. I drop to one knee as I quickly pat out a small flame at the hem of the white maiden dress I was shoved into.

Tom rests a hand on my shoulder. "Bree are you alright?"

"Yes, I'm okay. It's just everything they felt, I felt it too. It was very overwhelming and the strength it takes to look into the fire is incredible. I don't know how much of this I can take." I say, desperately trying to pull myself together.

"Bree this is what you are here for, to learn the truth. You are doing something no one else has ever done before. Focus. What did you see so far?"

"Two people from long ago, Mitace and Leandra. I thought they were lovers at first, but when he kissed her hand, she was almost horrified at the intimacy. I don't think this upper world had intimacy and they looked very young but mentioned a one-hundred-year anniversary from meeting, so I believe their time runs differently to ours."

"That's great, Bree. You are doing great. Are you ready to go back in?""

"Yes, I think I'm ready to try again." I say getting back to my feet. I look into the fire again, pushing the heat of the flames from my mind as the image of Mitace comes back into view.

Leandra and Mitace are sitting on the edge of a massive round crystal-clear lake. The water is so calm, it's the perfect mirror. Hundreds of people dressed in robes of brilliant white, sit around the edge to look up at the stars above. Time moves on while they watch the stars move and align so perfectly, until a planet slowly moves, rolling closer into view.

Everyone looks on in calm silence as the planet moves so close you would think it would touch the surface of the lake, but it doesn't. It rotates and moves backward, twisting through the sky, collecting the stars in its path. The sight is spectacular, but no sounds escape from a single mouth. There is only silence. Once the planet moves backward enough to be seen fully and it has collected the last star, it twinkles as it turns with such color and vibrance it's breathtaking.

The planet starts to slow its rotation. The light and position are perfectly viewed in the lake below now as everyone turns their attention to the mirror surface. It begins to ripple and move into a window that looks down to a huge celebration below.

Men and women dance around a massive fire on an island in the middle of a vast ocean. Pale blue people with skin that shimmers like diamonds are clapping and dancing at the surface of the water. Jubes glow and light the water for them as they all sing and play music all through the night, celebrating the wise ones and the balance of the lands.

Everyone has left the lake and gone to bed while Mitace and Leandra are the last ones remaining. "Do you ever wonder what it would be like to be down there celebrating with them?" Mitace asks Leandra.

"No, not really." she replies, dangling her feet just above the surface as they watch the last remaining couples dance around the fire.

"I do. I also wonder what is in those drinks they have that make them fall all over the place. It seems to make them think things are funnier too." Mitace says with a laugh.

Leandra laughs too. "Yes, they do have strange customs, don't they?"

There is only one couple still dancing around the fire now. The man grabs the woman and pulls her close to him turning the dance into a slow dance.

Mitace is mesmerized by them and Leandra becomes uncomfortable. "I think we should go now. I think the celebration has ended."

She moves to get up when Mitace grabs her hand, forcing a gasp from her lips. She looks at his hand wrapped around her wrist and calmly waits for Mitace to say whatever it is he was so desperate to say to her.

"Please stay with me."

His blue eyes and gentle words beg her to stay with him. He looks at her and realizes his hold on her wrist is not helping him at all, so he slowly releases her. Leandra stops for a moment and looks at the couple who have stopped dancing. She leans over and presses a small kiss to the man's cheek. He smiles and lifts his hand to where she just kissed him, then she turns and leaves. Leandra leans down to Mitace and does the same.

The flames push me out again, burning hotter. I scream, falling to my knees. "I'm sorry. I can't take it anymore! I just can't!" I scream. The pain is overwhelming me. I feel Tom rubbing at my back, trying desperately to help, as the pain sears through me.

"Think of Aiden. You can get through this." he says gently.

A painful wave hits me again. "Aiden!" I scream.

4

The Plan (Aiden)

That familiar pull hits me hard, knowing I am still connected to Bree, I do everything I can to slow my racing heart and desperately hope she knows I am still with her, no matter how useless I feel.

"What about the end of magic? If that rumor of the prophecy comes to pass, how can we defend ourselves?" someone asks.

Larna steps forward to answer. "Like I said before, no one but the judged will know the real truth until it's all over, but from what I have found from the prophets, magic will leave the land while the judgment is in progress."

"So, it will return once it's over?" another asks.

"We don't know. This is an event no one has done in hundreds of years. We do not have the answers. Please be patient." Larna urges.

Slowly we are able to usher the last of the people on to the waiting Oregrin's, leaving only a small group of us behind.

"Don't think I am accepting this in any way. I still have my fight to face; it will just have to wait for a while." Larna announces.

"For you to fight, you will have to produce your so-called princess to fight with you, otherwise you're just fighting a pointless battle." Madeline retorts.

"You are making a huge mistake." Larna hisses at Madeline.

"We have chosen our path. You need to come to terms with yours." Madeline sighs rolling her eyes.

"You will see Bree was never the chosen one to be judged." Larna retorts.

I laugh. "Ha, that's funny since your people just threw my bonded to her judgment, without knowing anything about what could happen to her or if she would even survive, and then you fight with us when we try to save her. You then tell us our Bree is an illegitimate lie, and every bit of rubbish you have uttered, needs to be adhered to without question. You may have everyone else wrapped around your rubbish, but you don't have me convinced." I retort.

"I never expected to convince anyone, and we were not amongst the others in the fight. We are a part of the ones who reside here." Larna snaps defensively.

"You mean you're a prophet?" I ask.

"In a way I guess I am, but more than anything this is my home. I watch overall."

"How come you're here then?"

"This is where I was raised, and this is where my father told me, we would find Bree someday. This place is very dear to me. With Bree and the king gone, I will be stepping forward to take care of our people until our princess returns. If there is anything you need, I will be only too happy to help. It was enlightening to meet you all." she says dryly and leaves on the next Oregrin.

"I really don't trust her. Things are just not right. There are too many questions, and she just rocks up out of nowhere." I grumble.

"Sounds off to me too." Roxy says.

"What are everyone's thoughts of Bree not being the king's daughter?" Roxy asks.

"I don't believe that for a second." I huff.

"But Bree having a sister sounds nice, don't you think?" Madeline smiles.

"Not if this sister was passed up for Bree. This sister could have it out for Bree. We don't know anything for a fact we just need to be careful." I advise.

"Okay, let's head back home and warn everyone." Roxy says grabbing my arm.

I flinch slightly at her contact but thankfully she does not notice. The whole time she has her hand on my arm the pain grows, until I am not listening to a word she is saying.

"So, what do you think?" she asks.

"Sounds like a plan. You all head back and I'll stay here."

"Wait, you can't stay behind. The kingdom needs you. Negalia needs you more than ever, with not knowing if the king is dead or alive, and if he is alive, we don't know where he is. Until we have more answers you are the new king Aiden and your people need you more than ever." Nathaniel says with an urgency in his voice.

"I don't want any changes here to go unreported and if...... I mean, when Bree comes out, I want to be here." I say firmly.

The ground vibrates beneath our feet as a tiny seedling pops up from the center of the platform and slowly begins to grow.

"What is going on?" Mac asks, trying to hide his concern.

"That has to be a good sign, don't you think?" Luc asks.

I look at the small seedling and hope the same.

Roxy steps forward. "I will stay behind and send word of any changes here. It looks like things will keep changing as Bree progresses. We have to think positive here. This must be a good sign and at this rate, it looks like Bree will be back at home with us soon. We have to stay positive."

I know she is right but leaving here without Bree is going to tear my heart out.

"I can't leave here yet anyway. I need time to let go of Logan. I'll be fine, you all need to go." Roxy says, tidying her high-top ponytail of golden-brown dreads.

We all look at her.

"We all need time to mourn our fallen friend, but he would say the same thing, when all this is over, we will have our chance to give him a send-off he would be proud of." Nathaniel says, placing his hand over his heart.

"Sounds like a plan. Don't chya get down and out now. I plan on given' em a send-off fit for a king don chya know!"

Although the fire is in his tone, the fire in his hair is so dull you can hardly see it anymore, and his orange eyes have lost their fire too. But even with his magic being drained from him, he still fights with passion.

"YEAH!!!" they all cheer.

A smile plays at the corner of my mouth.

"When do you plan on telling them about your injury?" my mother asks me in a low voice only I can hear.

"There is too much going on. I don't plan on telling anyone anything." I quietly reply.

She sighs as we get into the Oregrin's travel compartment.

Besides Metikye, who I insist stays behind with Roxy, I think a light task is best for him right now, the others all follow me.

We arrange that they will contact us with any progress or changes, and the others and I will save panic from erupting through the kingdom. We say our goodbyes and return home.

We have no time to rest when we return. The kingdom is in a panic. It takes a long time to calm the people down and set up ways to protect the kingdom and the flood of people seeking refuge.

When I finally get a chance to rest, I return to my room for some much-needed sleep. The moment I walk through the door, I forget how exhausted I am. Bree's lack of presence in the room is suffocating, every memory and moment we shared in here floods through my mind. The feelings tighten in my throat and in my chest. A few moments in this room have me turning on my heels and leaving. I move through the castle to the library.

With my father's passion for knowledge and imagination, he sought to gather books from all across the lands. He succeeded in creating the land's biggest and most famous library. It became Bree's second favorite place to come, and I realize it is no different here either.

It takes me a few tries before I give up on sleep and go for a walk. My stupid feet betray me, taking me past our training grounds where Bree continuously gave me little chance to outwit her as she always rose to my challenges, I continue to walk to the bloom tree, Bree, and my place, our bond is the strongest here. I sigh and rest my forehead to the tree.

"By the elements, Bree, you will never know how much I miss you." I declare to the tree.

"Aiden!" Bree's voice calls to me.

My head snaps up. "Bree?" How can it be her? Am I losing my mind?

"Aiden!" Bree calls to me again.

It is not just my imagination! "Bree!" I call out to her over and over, but she does not call out my name again.

"Aiden?" my mother calls to me, snapping me out of my insane chatter to a damn tree.

I swear a few moments without Bree, and I am losing my mind. "Yes Mother?" I say, quickly composing myself.

"You need to get that arm looked at. I know you're playing it off."

"I told you to drop it!" I snap, getting irritated. It is not completely about the arm, but I'm in no mood at the moment for anything. I sink down, pressing my back to the tree.

"Take your shirt off." she presses.

I sigh and do as she asks knowing she will not shut up until I do, not that she can do much as an Akuma anyway. She gasps when I remove my shirt, revealing the burn mark on my arm.

"How did this happen?" she asks.

I lean my head back against the tree. "Just before we met up with you, Bree and I were gathering prillum vines in the capium fields. I pulled one down and lost my footing. It's just a little burn from a capium crystal, I'll be fine." I say brushing off her worries.

"Aiden this is not little, capium spreads and this burn looks to be doing just that. It needs to be treated and soon." she says.

"Did you tell Bree?" she asks.

"No, it didn't hurt that much before, so I didn't think it was worth mentioning, still don't, come to think of it." I say, shrugging.

"I am an Akuma! This happened because of capium! You don't know what will happen and I swear if you don't take this more seriously, I'll take this out of your control. I will tell everyone and make you listen to me!" she yells.

I sigh. "Fine. What is the plan then?" I ask, placing my hands behind my head, making myself comfortable.

"Plan? I....I....I don't have a plan." she confesses.

I smile. "That is what I thought. You go off on a screaming fit with no idea what you are asking of me. Let me enlighten you a little Mother, I plan to keep the kingdom from falling apart, I plan on getting my bonded home as soon as I can, and I plan on making sure I am alive when that day comes, so... I have found that while magic is disappearing from the land, we need to find something that will heal this burn without magic." I answer smugly.

"How are we going to find something like that?" she asks, a little calmer now.

"I already have, but I still don't know where to find it. I've asked Nathaniel to track the location down for me."

"And that would be what?"

I roll my eyes at her continuous bombardment of questions.

"It is a powerful healing moss I remember Bree telling me about, so the plan is to find it and get some answers."

5

The Way Things Are

"Aiden?"

I know I felt him just now, the feeling was so strong. I'm positive I heard him call my name. I push the pain away, forcing back the fire. Aiden is with me. I know he is. I can do this. Slowly, I push myself back onto my feet. Tom is still rubbing my back.

"That's it! Think of Aiden. You can do this Bree!" he says, cheering me on, pushing me not to give up.

The fire shows Leandra kneeling at an altar chanting with a room full of others. The sound echoes around the temple. I can see the clean white walls, and the polished floors reflect the faces of those on their knees.

Mitace walks into the temple and stands at the back. He stop's himself from going any further. Mitace just stands and watches the others chant on the polished floor.

After a few moments, another man walks in. Noticing Mitace at the entrance, he inclines his head and gives his hand a wave for him to go first. Shaking out of his thoughts, Mitace moves to a spot on the floor and slowly bows his head to the floor as the man follows beside him.

Mitace rests his forehead to the cool floor. He's not chanting but seems to be in deep thought. Others have finished and left. It's only when Leandra comes up to him that he snaps out of his thoughts.

"You were not chanting, are you feeling alright?" she asks him.

"Yes...um ...no I guess I'm not feeling myself today."

"That is strange as we don't get sick. I wonder what the problem could be."

Mitace looks around and notices Leandra and he are the only ones left in the temple now.

"I don't feel sick, I feel...I don't know how to explain it... I... I don't want to chant the same chant we chant every day. I don't want to do the same things we have done for thousands of years. I don't know why I feel this way, but I do know I feel better when I am with you." Mitace confesses.

"Wisdom and balance, there is no birth, no death, no sickness, no love or hate, envy or malice, we are balance, and that is what the lands need from us, Mitace. If you are having these.... feelings, we must tell the wise ones right away. I don't think this is a good thing."

"Please Leandra. I'm sorry. I don't know what came over me. I feel much better. Just forget what I said, okay?"

She looks at him for a moment. "Very well, but promise me, if you feel like that again you will speak to the wise ones." She looks at him with large pleading eyes.

Mitace gives her his best show-stopping smile. "Of course, I will." he replies.

She smiles in return, pleased with his answer. Mitace gets up and leaves the temple.

Mitace's smile falls the moment he is away from Leandra. His blue robes move around his ankles as he walks to the viewing room. The room is empty and the pool is still reflecting the island below. Mitace sits at the water's edge, watching the underlings below.

Instead of chanting in the temple, he returns to the viewing pool every day. Mitace becomes so engrossed, one day he doesn't notice Leandra sit beside him.

"So, this is where you have been of late." she says, making Mitace jump. Her eyes go wide at his reaction. "What is with you lately?"

"I'm sorry, I really was not paying attention. You startled me that's all." Not thinking, Mitace places his hand over Leandra's as he speaks. Leandra sucks in a deep breath. Mitace notices what he has done but seems to decide not to show any care.
Leandra stays frozen for a few moments, deciding what to say and do. Just as it seems she is going to say something, Mitace speaks. He is still holding onto her hand. He looks down into the viewing pond.

"Every day they get up to go to the fields. They take care of the families, laugh, cry, get sick. It's strange, but I think...how does death even work? An old man died yesterday, and they all leaked from their eyes and called it crying. To die is to sleep in a box under the dirt. I don't see why they don't just wake him up, then they won't leak anymore, but they did something to a young girl who got sick and died. They burned her body to ashes. I really didn't understand that." Mitace says, scrunching his eyebrows up. "Today I watched the two people we saw dancing together that night of the celebration, dance at another celebration. Everything was white with lots of flowers. They held hands under an arch of them, too, and said wonderful things to each other. A lot of people leaked again. It was a very confusing moment."

Leandra looks at the viewing pool, a little confused. "They cry when they're happy and sad?"

"Yes, it seems that way. They are very interesting. Not a moment goes by that something new does not intrigue me. Look over there!" Mitace says excitedly, pointing to a man working on a boat whistling.

"What am I looking at?" Leandra asks.

"That man was yelling at his family the other day that he slaves away in a job he hates, just to put a roof over their heads, clothes on their backs, and food in their bellies. I saw the mother prepare the food and dress the children, then once he's away from the house, he's whistling working on that flotation device. He does not look to hate the job at all. I don't understand how that one works."

Leandra seems to have forgotten Mitace still has her hand trapped under his. She is hanging on his every word.

"How do they function with such contradictions?" she asks.

"Honestly, I do not know, but it is wonderful watching them. The small people, they call children and the smallest ones they call babies. But it gets confusing when they spoke of the large lady having a baby but she held no such thing."

"I have heard of birth before that is how they multiply. The wise one told me that. Before you become a wise one, you must visit the world below to learn all you can, to pass your knowledge on."

Mitace snaps his head up to look at her. "There is a way to visit the land below?"

"I believe so, that is what the wise one said after all."

Excitedly, Mitace jumps up, releasing Leandra's hand. "I have to go ask the wise ones how this is done!" Mitace moves quickly to the door, leaving Leandra shocked and confused as to what just happened.

Mitace goes to a big temple with big pearl doors and raps on the door. Almost immediately, the doors open. Mitace steps inside onto the polished marble floor. Only the light padding of his bare feet is heard through the long hall. Mitace keeps walking until he gets to a large door that opens as he nears.

"Mitace!" a loud voice speaks to him. He looks around but doesn't see anyone.

"What has brought you to us today Mitace?" the voice calls.

"I have come to ask about...the dwellers below."

"Mitace, curiosity is not a trait found in our people. If not dealt with this could cause imbalance." the voice calls.

"I don't wish to cause panic. I only wish to satisfy my questions to grow my knowledge."

The voice goes quiet for a few moments. "What are the questions you seek answers to?"

"I wish to visit the dwellers below to learn, so one day I might become as wise." The silence is long and deafening as Mitace patiently waits for some sign his words have been heard.

"You are far younger than any we have sent before. Everything always has its time." The voice says. Startling Mitace.

"With all due respect, have any before me been as interested as I, to ask such a thing? And do you think waiting so many years with unanswered questions could cause an imbalance? I am experiencing strange feelings and I think if you send me now, I will find my balance again."

"Mitace, I do hope you understand why we can't send you. If you cannot find your balance here, you most certainly won't be able to find balance down there. That is the reason we cannot let you go." the wise one gently replies.

"All I want is to ask my questions and get my answers. After that I will find my balance; I will find peace in my fate. How else would you suggest I find my balance?"

"Mitace, please listen carefully. You cannot go if you have not been chosen to be a wise one, as the underlings' way of life is dangerous in the hands of those not centered enough to come back from it. I'm sorry, Mitace, but you are not a chosen one, nor are you centered enough to learn from the experience. Your questions and your curiosity are dangerous, especially if you think our way of life is something you must find peace in to endure. We suggest you forget about everything and let things go back as they should. You will find no answers down there, only more questions and it will only corrupt your light."

Mitace sees clearly there is no way to convince them and talking to them was a big mistake. "Yes, of course. I don't know what I was thinking. Of course, you are right. I am sorry to have worried you and wasted your time. Thank you for your guidance." Mitace says. He bows his head and leaves.

6

Swamp Forgotten (Aiden)

A sharp pounding stirs me from my sleep. I get precious little since Bree has been gone. That damn pounding echoes through the room again. I growl loudly.

"What is it? This better be good!" I yell.

The door swings open and Nathaniel strides in, not even fazed with my mood. Not that it surprises me.

"Quit your bellyaching, at least I knocked this time." he says with a chipper smile.

"Last time I was with Bree!" I snap, throwing a pillow at him.

Nathaniel shrugs me off again, dodging the pillow with ease. "Oh, are we playing teenage girl games where we have pillow fights and braid each other's hair?" he jibes playfully, clapping his hands like a child.

I sigh, not having the energy to rip into him the way I usually would.

"Get up, get dressed. We have a journey to plan." he says.

I sit upright. "You found it?"

"Of course!" He replies indignantly. "I am offended you have so little faith in my abilities." he taunts jokingly.

I cannot help but smile a little. "Thank you."

"No big deal. I chased some leads to a very remote part of the outer kingdoms. What you want has the highest chance of growing in the swamplands off the border." he says.

"How long will it take to get there?" I ask.

"If we take andocrits we will be there in two or three days. The real problem is finding the moss you are after when we get there." he replies. "Do you even have a clue what it looks like? Because no one I have spoken to has ever seen it before, it's all mostly stories."

I pull Bree's book out of my bedside drawer. "Bree told me about it a while ago. The moss she spoke about is right here in her book." I open the book, flicking through the back pages where I find what I am looking for. "This is what we are searching for." I say, showing him a picture of what looks like a blended looking patch of red, yellow, and orange mossy carpet.

"Okay, this helps a lot. So, we know where and now what we are looking for, let us get the team together and get moving. We should only take a small team with us, with all the chaos at the moment we might need some guys you trust to stay back and watch over things here." he says.

"That is exactly what I was thinking. Luc, Mac, you, and my mother should be all we need for the trip. I'll leave Metikye, Madeline, and Roxy behind to look after things here while we are away." I confirm.

"Is it wise to leave Madeline behind? The kingdom might not be as accepting of your words if you are gone. She did just come back from being on the run after poisoning the lillulian orchard."

"After everyone was told what had happened to the king, their queen and that she acted on her queen's orders she could not be judged for anything they themselves would have done if their queen had asked of them. Not to mention, with the queen's return that in itself has been a big deal."

"I guess you are right, but we still have the problem that Metikye and Roxy are still at the Maiden, aren't they?" he asks.

"No, I already sent a furngra to call them back. With everything going on we need all the hands we can get, and I am confident now that I will know of any changes with Bree before anyone else." I reply. Nathaniel gives me a quizzical look. "I haven't given up on Bree, far from it, I just feel if there is any change I will know. I cannot explain it, but I feel it, I do not need them there. I need them here. Can you just accept that, and stop riding me over every little thing?" I growl.

Nathaniel shakes his head for a moment and I think he is not going to let this go. "All right if, you are sure. I am just worried about you, we all are. Bree is getting through this, and you need to be in good form for when she comes home." he says.

I cannot help but smile. "Nathaniel, I plan on doing just that. I'll burn this place to the ground before I let her go."

The sun has only started to rise when we get out to the courtyard.

Luc is stretching, and yawning, while Mac is bellyaching about his morning pick me up. I do not know what he has in that thing nor do I want to know, as long as it does the trick, I don't give a damn but, in the mornings, his extra six years on me shows, especially when he is next to Luc, the youngest in our team at only twenty-two.

"Mac, Luc, are you both ready to head out? Do you even own a brush Luc? That nest looks angry." I say, poking fun at his messy blond hair that looks like he just stepped out of bed.

"I refuse to grace that with an answer, and for your information we will soon be ready to depart. Roxy and Metikye should be here any moment." he replies, scratching at his stomach.

"Roxy and Metikye are already here you mean." she calls over the top as she walks over to us.

"It's good to see you, Roxy." I say with a smile.

"You too."

"Someone has to handle things while you are away, looks like these two are not going to be much help." Roxy says as Mac and Luc yawn again.

"Hey, some people need sleep to live. It's not our fault you're not normal." Mac retorts rubbing at his dark brown locks sleepily.

Roxy pretends to stab herself in the heart with an invisible knife in mock insult. "He is taking the two of you to keep you out of trouble." Roxy retorts back.

"All right that's enough. I thought I was working with professionals, not children." I scold.

"Hey, we were only lightning the mood Aiden, relax." replies Roxy.

"I will relax when Bree is safe at home with me, until then, we need to keep the kingdom safe. "Any changes at the maiden?" I ask changing the subject.

Roxy shakes her head mournfully. "Besides the seedling growing out of control nothing has changed."

Where is Metikye?" I ask, looking around for him.

"He is with Madeline. She is feeding him and getting him settled in. He really has not been handling the lack of magic very well, but I think I have done a good job keeping him together. I think most of the magical people are going to be struggling. Metikye says we should set some things up for them because he is almost certain we will get a flood of people asking for help to get by. None of them know how to protect their people with no magic." Roxy replies.

"We have already had a flood of people come. People are acting out because magical leaders are who they rely on to protect them, without that they will lose order."

"We have the same system here, but most of our abilities are focused on training, not magic. There is a little to get started but after a while, it is all in the training. The kings of my land have always been taught that magic can be a strength or a weakness depending on how you use it. So, we have always strengthened both to keep order in any circumstance, and it looks like they were right." I say, prouder of my lineage than ever. Although if Bree ever knew about that part of me, I wonder if she would still love me, or would she run from me? Thankfully Roxy puts an end to my uninvited thought.

"Well right now we need to get you all off to this swamp land, find what we need, and get back here fast. We are in desperate times." Roxy says authoritatively.

"All right everyone let's mount up and get going." I say, moving to my andocrit Anzibar. I give him a brief affectionate pat on his forehead, he moves his tatted wing as I move around to his side, to help me up on to his strong back, I pause for a moment to untangle one of his matted dreads from my brown leather boot. The moment I am on, he rises to his feet. I look over to find Nathaniel, and the others are ready and making their way over to me. I look down to Roxy. "I know the kingdom is in good hands, should you need us...."

"Hey this isn't my first time on the job you know." she cuts me off, crossing her arms.

I smile. "All right we are off then."

We have made good time in our journey to the swamplands, with no thanks to my mother. Not to mention with her illusion I still know her spikes are there, and I am the one obviously stuck carrying her after her andocrit went crazy. The illusion may be in place, but they obviously know what she currently is. I sigh.

"What are you sighing about? You haven't said much to me this entire trip." my mother whines.

"Bree needs to come back soon and get this damn cure made for you because I'm well and truly over those spikes of yours, not to mention our kingdom needs you and you're not much help as you are."

"Our kingdom has gotten along just fine with you leading them. I know your father would be as proud as I am, even if your father and I found our way back to each other and a cure returned me to my former self, I doubt we would take back the throne. You have taken over for far too long to be temporary and our people have already accepted you. If we came back, it would only cause confusion."

"I don't know why we are even talking about this." I say, trying to end this conversation.

"Then what would you like to talk about? I'm bored and I don't even know why you brought me along."

"I brought you so you could put your nose to work." I say a little amused.

"I beg your pardon?" the queen snorts.

"You heard me. If you have to be an Akuma, might as well use it to our advantage." I say, brushing off her irritation.

"I thought that was what Nathaniel was for." she huffs.

"We will find it far quicker if you both work together."

She sighs, resting her head back onto her front two paws.

"I tell you Bree did a trip far longer than this one with you and I don't know how she did it. Not only does my body hurt from this damn box saddle but my brown leather pants are riding so far up my back side I can almost taste the leather, plus Anzibar has never had to deal with this kind of thing before."

"I always thought if given the choice you would pick this andocrit over any of us. Every chance you got as a boy you were on this thing."

"Anzibar never expected anything of me, Mother, and we have seen and done many great things together, and I don't see how you can complain, you are the one that bought him for me. You said I never appreciated what I had, then you say I appreciated him too much. Can't have it both ways." I say, getting irritated.

Before my mother can retort, Nathaniel calls out to us from in front. *Thank the elements.* I move us to his side and see what he is pointing to. It is a sign overgrown with vines and grass, but you can see the words, *swamp forgotten* in dirty black lettering.

"Okay, here we go. Let's stick together. No one knows what is out here so be careful." Nathaniel nods his head moving us on.

"Are you getting off here for a walk?" I ask my mother.

"Sure can, I think a good stretch will be good for both of us." she says, obviously getting irritated by my lack of stimulating conversation.

"I agree." I say, equally irritated.

I go to set Anzibar down so she can get off, when she stands and leaps off his back, bounding off a few nearby trees until she reaches the ground quite impressively.

"You say I'm supposed to sniff this thing out yet I have no idea what it smells like."

I roll my eyes, pull out Bree's book and open it to the page I marked. "Bree's book says the smell is very distinct to sensitive noses. It has a sweet lillulian scent, with a rotten oregrin flesh smell."

"Oh joy, that sounds very inviting." she replies dryly.

We move through the swamplands for hours. The light is leaving the sky quickly.

"I think we need to set up camp before we lose all light." I say tiredly.

Mac and Luc nod in agreement. Nathaniel finds a clear enough spot for the night. Long after the sun has gone down, Luc lights a fire and Mac sets up some food while I unpack the blankets.

After feeding and watering the andocrits, we sit around the fire eating a stew Madeline brewed for our trip. It tastes quite good, and I can see everyone else is enjoying it. Since we brought her back, Madeline has not talked much, she just spends her time in the kitchen. Luc is staring at his food in deep thought.

"What's on your mind Luc?" I ask.

"Not much, yet everything."

"Anything you want to talk about?"

"No, not really. If you want to talk, we can talk about you and Bree?"

"And why would Bree be our topic of conversation?"

"I don't know, sounds like an interesting topic to me."

"Really? Well, if we are discussing interesting topics, I think your real name would be a great topic." I say with a smirk.

Luc gives me a scowl and Mac laughs. Luc never lets anyone know his name. We have all tried guessing but no one has gotten it right.

"A guessing game sounds fun, but what if we get it right but you lie about your name?" I ask.

Luc looks at all of us and shakes his head. "All hell breaks loose and you all have nothing better to do than pick on me for my name, by the elements we are in trouble, aren't we?"

"Come on Luc, it's a bit of fun." Mac says, egging things on.

"Whatever, I don't care."

"Lucifer?" Mac asks.

"No."

"Luca?"

"No."

"Lucasta?"

Luc just scrunches his nose up. One by one we throw names around the campfire.

"Lucy?"

"Lucilla?"

"Lucinda?"

"Lucas?"

Name after name is rejected, until the names stop and all that can be heard is the sound of soft snores. I move over to my mother who seems to be snoring the loudest. She is curled up near the fire. I drop a blanket over her as I smile to myself, she is so exhausted she does not stir. Anzibar is curled up fast asleep too. I slide down his side and watch over them all as they sleep.

7

Pushing Boundaries

Leandra is waiting outside, pacing up and down and picking at her cuticles when she notices Mitace. She seems relieved but her concern returns when she sees his face.

"Are you... angry?" she asks.

"They won't let me go. They said I will never be a wise one. They said I have no center and I will never find my balance if I go or chase after any of my questions, I will only corrupt my light."

"They are the wise ones. Who are we to question? If they say it's best to leave this alone then that is what must be done." Leandra says, trying to comfort Mitace, but the effect is quite the opposite.

"There is more to this world than doing the same thing for the rest of eternity. I never ask questions. If there is something, I want to know. I am not going to stop until I get my answers. Come on Leandra, you cannot truly feel that way. I know you have questions just as I do. I know you have enjoyed holding hands and doing different things. I know it, so why do you deny it? How can you be truly centered if you are lying to yourself?"

"Because I find my balance in knowing when something is taking me down a destructive path. Mitace if you continue this way, I don't think they will be as understanding." she says, her words dripping with concern.

"I'll teach everyone this is not as we are supposed to live. This cannot be all there is to life. I want to experience love, happiness, sadness. I know I'm angry and you know...it actually feels good."

"Mitace you're scaring me." she says, taking a step back from him.

"How about I show you one thing? If you do not think it's wonderful, I'll stop asking questions." Mitace says. He holds out his hand to her.

A battle is clearly waging on in her head. There is the promise of hopefully saving him from a dark path or possibly falling into one herself. "No, Mitace. I do not want you to get hurt. I know I'm not centered right now and that does not excite me, it scares me, so from now on you are on your own." she turns from him, but as she starts to walk away, Mitace grabs her arm.

"Don't leave me." he hisses.

"All you did was ensure I do." she says, pulling her arm from his grip.

A few people have gathered, and start whispering amongst themselves. Leandra takes this chance to leave without further protesting from Mitace.

"If anyone has questions, please follow me." Mitace says, raising his hands out to everyone in a calm gesture.

The flames push me back. The fire is burning so hot now it is getting harder to calm the flames long enough to see anything.

"Are you okay, Bree?" Tom asks me.

"Yes, I will be fine. I just need a few moments to gather myself again. It is getting intense in there."

"The flames?"

"No, the vision. Mitace is really going down a bad road, and I am starting to see where this might be going, but just as I think I have things figured out something new comes out, turning everything upside down. I'm giving it everything I have to stay on my feet."

"Bree you are the strongest person I know. Mia can't kill me for saying that because she would say the same." Tom says pushing a strand of my hair behind my ear.

"You have something here that you need to know. I have no doubt you were the only one to ever see this and the only one it was ever intended for. I feel it as strongly as my love for Mia."

I look at Tom and see in his eyes that he really does believe in what he is saying. I sigh in defeat. "Don't worry I might need to catch my breath a few times, but I won't give up. I promise." I say, giving him my best champion-I-can-do-this smile.

Tom laughs. "That's our girl." Toms says with such love and honesty it gives me the renewed boost I needed.

The flames have settled again. The viewing window shows a gathering of people in robes, in front of a massive white stage with large columns surrounding the space. Leandra is far from Mitace, who seems to be with people who are whispering and acting up a little at the back, making others look at them in annoyance.

Leandra does not smile or seem her normal self, nor does she acknowledge the behavior behind her.

"We have gathered everyone here today to discuss a disturbance in the balance of things." The crowd looks over to the group making hushed comments in the back.

"We are giving you the chance to come to us if you have any questions or need to discuss anything upsetting your balance." A wise one encourages at the front in robes of brilliant white.

"Ha!" a voice in the back scoffs.

"Answer questions?"

"Help?" another, remarks sarcastically.

"That's a laugh, isn't it!"

"You don't answer questions, you want us to forget about them and leave it alone."

Leandra seems surprised when several voices speak these words, and not one of them is Mitace.

"Yeah!" the group replies in unison.

"What are you going to do, send us down if we don't stop asking questions?" another man calls out.

"No!" the voice booms, shocking everyone to silence. "This is the only warning that will be given. We cannot live with the dwellers below, as we are a danger to their world, and in the wrong hands could destroy them all and send their world off balance and into chaos. The only thing we can do is imprison you until you are not a danger any longer or...... we extinguish your light."

The chatter erupts. It is so loud and clear panic is on so many faces. Mitace does not speak or show any concern. Leandra looks at him. Their eyes meet, and strangely, Mitace is the one to turn away first. The wise one leaves as the talk continues. Mitace's group walks out, still talking. She raises her hood to cover her face. She moves in with the rest of Mitace's group.

Over forty people in white robes weave in and out of the woods. The light has left the sky and the stars dance across the treetops. The air is soft, and a sweet smell of flowers drift across the gentle wind that ruffles Leandra's hood. Her cloak puffs and weaves, catching in the wind. She draws it tighter, determined not to be seen. They walk deeper into the trees until a large cliff comes into view. Vines cover the base, and a long way up, one by one they disappear behind the vines.

Leandra follows them and does the same. Behind the vines they come away from the cliff face enough to walk around. The group has stopped for a moment. A little way up they begin to walk again. When Leandra gets up further, she turns into an opening into the cliff. They all travel silently through the long dark passage that is lit by a large candle Mitace holds.

Leandra follows them all into a large opening filled with bright crystals that light the whole cavern. Beds and chairs are strewn all over the floor. Leandra ducks to a side passage just as the last of them enter, taking off the cloaks and strewing them over designated spots they each seem to have set up for themselves.

"Is anyone worried about what the wise one said?" a woman says, breaking the silence.

"If you're getting scared you shouldn't have come back here." A young man bite back at her.

"I'm not saying I'm scared. I thought this was all about asking questions. That just happens to be a question I'm interested in asking." she retorts.

"They will try to reform us first. You heard them they're trying to scare us."

"Honestly, after the things I have learned here, can you really forget?" a man asks the room.

The people in the room all look at each other. One by one, they shake their heads or say 'no' in almost a whisper. They all direct their gaze to Mitace at the front of the room, where he is sprawled out on a large throne-like chair silently listening to the conversation unfold.

Mitace looks at the crowd of faces waiting for him to say something. He sits up a little. "You are all welcome to do as you please, but I'm not going to stop finding my answers. If I have to seek them quietly or have my light extinguished if they deem it fit, someday I'll take that, for I would rather live my life the way I choose than spend the rest of eternity living in the dark."

The group of people all nod in agreeance cheering, "Yes!"

"Let them try and do their worst. You could see they were not happy more of us were asking questions."

"So Mitace, what are you going to teach us today?" a man asks.

"Yes what?" the room bustles with chatter.

"Enough!" Mitace says, hushing them instantly. "There is not a lot left I haven't already told you."

"Can you tell us more of intimacy?" a man asks near the front. He's huddled up with a dark-haired woman on a bean bag looking mattress on the floor. The dark-haired woman snuggles up to him in agreement.

"Yes, kissing is fun and holding hands. What else do they do?" she asks.

Mitace gets up from his chair and strides over to the woman. He leans down and gently glides his fingers down the curve of her neck, to her breasts. The woman's breath hitches, and her eyes grow heavy. She lets out a small moan. As everyone watches in awe, one by one the men copy the act on their female partner.

"At this point simply continue to touch your partner where it feels good."

"Can you show us?" someone asks.

"There is only one person I would want to try the rest with, and she isn't here." he says with a sigh.

"Why isn't she here? I'm sure if she knew the truth she would be here."

"It is not as easy as that. You saw for yourself today there are many that will never understand us and stand in our way for the truth."

Mitace strolls over to the large rock pool in the center of the room. He touches the water and images of dwellers below appear in its waters.

"Any questions you have about the dwellers can be found in the rock pool."

A rustle comes from the back of the room where a tall brown-haired man has Leandra by the arm, pushing her to the front where Mitace stands. Mitace's eyes grow wide when he sees its Leandra.

"What are you doing here?" he asks her.

"I was worried about you. I came to make sure you were alright, and I walk into this! Mitace this is not going to help any of you."

"You were worried about me? Do not make me laugh! You said I was on my own. Tell the truth. You were spying on us!" he says, bearing down on her threateningly.

Leandra shrinks a little "No! After they said you could be imprisoned or your light extinguished, I got worried about you."

"Scared you mean?" Mitace corrects her cockily.

"Is it scared? I do not know, but the feeling is not pleasant at all." She remarks rubbing at her chest.

Mitace seems amused by her honesty. "So, you care about me?"

"Of course, I care about you. Why would you ask such a thing?"

"No, you are exhibiting actions of a person who more than cares for someone in the way we are taught to care for one another. This is a feeling you reserve for liking one person more than any other."

"I don't understand what you are trying to say Mitace."

"Leandra, there are forty other people in this room all doing the same thing, but your worry is reserved mostly for me, isn't it?"

Leandra goes pale as she realizes what Mitace is trying to convey to her. "Leandra, what I feel for you is love. I know it is. I know you feel something for me too. You simply will not admit it. I do not want to live a life without you, but you are asking me to choose. In the life I want with you, we would be experiencing everything we are being denied but you only want to follow the system of things."

"I look to the world below and see how free they all are. They don't know the struggles we face up here."

"They look up to us because we keep the worlds in balance, we are too great for their world."

"What does that even mean?"

"I don't know but they should never know us. We are to always watch over them, it is our destiny and our duty."

"I'm just so sick of it all! We spend every day dedicating our lives to make their lives better but not our own. We live and breathe to serve them, are you not even a little resentful?"

"No, why would I be? I think of them as children we have to watch over and protect them. There is no greater thing in life than watching your children grow and succeed."

"What if we could have children and live the way they do, fall in love? Be more than we are here."

Her face falls as she takes a step back, away from him.

"What are you talking about? This is mad talk. This is not who we are or what we are about. We are order and wisdom through the worlds. Talk like this will end only one way. I will not go down that path with you Mitace."

Mitace steps towards her, fear and anger spread across his face. "One way or the other Leandra, I will open your eyes to what they are keeping from us. If you will not come to me willingly, I will take you by force. There is no way I'm going anywhere without you!" Mitace threatens, throwing Leandra to the cushion-covered floor.

"Mitace please stop! You are scaring me!" Leandra cries trying to scramble away from him.

"Oh, now you acknowledge fear?" he taunts sarcastically grabbing her legs, pulling her back to him roughly.

The room is silent, watching intently as the scene escalates.

Impatiently Mitace slams Leandra's wrists above her head. Throwing a leg over, he straddles Leandra, pinning her body to the floor. Mitace puts both her hands in one of his, freeing his other hand to move over her robes, pushing them free from her body and exposing her to him. Leandra struggles as hard as she can against his heavy weight holding her down. She screams for Mitace to stop but he only covers her mouth with his own.

The room does not move or say a single thing. No one questions Mitace or tries to help Leandra, they only watch on, enthralled and eager to see more.

Mitace's hand trails down forcing his way between her thighs, forcing his way through her attempts to prevent his unwelcome intrusion. Finding her entrance, he slowly pushes his way in, forcing muffled cries from her. Mitace continues his intrusion while slowly adding more and more to the assault until he can move more freely.

After he has spent more than enough time preparing her, he breaks the kiss. Breathing heavy, he retracts his hand to rifle and pull at his own robes, undressing himself. Leandra's eyes grow wide, fear etched in every feature. Mitace holds her firmly as tears begin to fall from her eyes.

"Please...don't...do...this." she whimpers. Her fight almost all gone from exhaustion.

Mitace freezes as he places himself at her entrance. After forcing his way between her shaking thighs, he lowers his head and kisses a tear from her cheek. She looks at him with hope that he will finally see reason.

"I can't live another moment without you Leandra, If I stop now nothing will ever change. Weather you hate me or not, at least this way, we will go down together." he says. Slamming into her, abruptly forcing his way through her body's resistance.

My stomach tightens and I can't look any longer. I fall to my knees as her screams tear through me. I empty the contents of my stomach, retching and heaving long after there is nothing left. Tom is rubbing at my back trying to calm me.

"What the hell happened in there?" Tom exclaims in a panic.

"I can't believe he would do that to her!" I cry desperately, letting my tears flood my face. I can't stop them as they fall, soaking the front of my white dress.

"Did what? Bree! You have to talk to me! What happened?"

"Mitace...he couldn't bear being parted from Leandra. She denied him. He lost it and took her! Right there in front of them all! More than forty of them! And not one of them tried to help her!"

"I don't understand. What are you talking about?" Tom frantically asks, trying to make sense of my crying rampage of nonsensical words.

Slowly I take a few moments to calm myself down a little. When I feel I can get my words out clearly, I lift my head to look at Tom. I'm trying not to show how utterly disgusted and sick I feel right now, but fail completely. The words tumble from my mouth.

"In front of a room full of people, Mitace let them all watch as he defiled her!"

8

Strange Object (Aiden)

I wake abruptly, feeling so sick I could vomit. At that precise moment I notice Luc hovering over me. Startled, I shoot up. My heart is racing. "Is everything all right?" I ask, trying to get my bearings.

"Sorry to wake you like this, but you have to see this."

Quickly, I move to my feet, lacing my black leather boots and tucking in my thick white shirt into my brown leather pants.

The sun is only starting to rise. Most of the surrounding area is still engulfed in a thick fog. The smell of the morning mildew is strong and covers the space, giving the area a chill. Slowly, Luc leads me to a small moss-covered mound not too far from camp.

"What is this? You woke me up for a mound?"

"No, it looks like one but it's not."

We move around it to find a small opening.

"What is that?" I ask.

"I don't know, I was scouting the area last night but when I went up the top of what I thought was a mound to get some height, my foot slipped and a strip of moss came off. I got down to have a closer look and found under it was a strange metal. I ran to Nathaniel but Mac told me they had left hours before, so I asked Mac to see if he had any ideas. We stripped more moss off until a large enough section revealed a strangely shaped door."

"Well?"

"We still have no idea. It looks like a metal house, come see."

Luc leads me to the part they have freed of moss and opens the door. Inside it smells damp and moldy and of something else that is far from pleasant, but unlike anything I have ever smelled before.

"Isn't it a bit small for a house?" I move forward, peaking my head further inside.

"This entire thing is made of metal. The number of weapons and armor you could get out of this is incredible."

"Let's take shifts uncovering this whole thing."

"We were hoping you would say that." Luc says gleefully.

For the rest of the day, we remove the moss to uncover the object hiding underneath.

"Reina has been gone for quite a while do you think she is alright?" Mac asks.

"She is with Nathaniel. I'm sure they are fine. We did say if they go far to turn back when the sun hits the topmost point, if they did, they should not be back for another two hours yet." I say trying to defuse his worries.

The object is completely uncovered now. It looks like a small home, with a small, long bed in the back and two chairs in the front.

"I have never seen such soft chairs before." I say, gliding my hand across the soft fabric. "I can't understand the thin, strangely shaped table in front of the see-through wall, and why have it so far away from the table? How could you eat off of it? Your head would bump the see-through wall. I want to know why there is a big wheel in front of the left side." I move around the object and notice something under it. I begin to dig around the bottom. "What in the name of magic is this? Mac come look at this!" I gesture for Mac and Luc to come and see what I have found. "Look it has these strange things by my feet that move a little, and little wheels on this thing in the front look like they move."

"Whatever for?"

"If they don't do anything, do you think they are something for distracting a child?"

"Could be, are you thinking this could be an armored carriage of some kind?"

"It is beginning to look that way."

"If that is the case what in the name of magic could be so valuable for the need of such a thing to protect it? Not even royalty have something like this when traveling."

"I really don't know Mac, but for some strange reason I feel a personal connection with it." I say absentmindedly.

"You? How?" Mac asks me, a little taken back by my confession.

"I know it sounds strange, but it has a Bree feel to it. I really feel like she will know what this is."

"Out of all the things I would think you strange for saying, funnily enough this is not one of them, as I think of it, I would think Bree too."

The sun has gone down and now we are all getting worried. There has been no sign of Nathaniel or my mother.

"Luc, Mac, you both should get some sleep. At the first light we will go look for them." I say regretfully.

"I agree. I don't trust this place at all." Mac says, shaking his shoulders as if shaking off a chilling thought.

Mac confirms my suspicions when he refuses my offer of me taking the first shift and in the end, I give up trying.

"You did most last night. You are not doing that again. You cannot help anyone if you are tired, and you have not been looking good these last couple of days anyway."

I look at him, trying to gauge my chances of him backing down and find I will waste more energy than I have, arguing with him.

I incline my head, accepting I will not be on first shift and move over to Anzibar who lays down as I get nearby. It does not take long for me to fall asleep with Anzabar's warmth at my back, my exhaustion catching up to me.

I am startled awake as something crawls across my ankle. It is still dark and the fog is thick. The embers from the fire are glowing enough to still be seen through the fog. I look around, trying to see the others. Slowly, I get up, shaking my foot to make sure what crawled over my ankle is gone. Anzibar is still asleep at my back and as I move closer to the fire, I can just make out Luc sleeping. A rustle from behind Luc has me on edge.

I slowly move closer to the bush with one hand on my sheath and the other ready to draw my sword if need be. A twig snaps just as I reach the bush. Mac stumbles out of it backward with his backside bare.

"Ah! By the wise ones!" Mac frantically yells.

"Man cover that thing up!" I say, causing Mac to jump and tumble over his black pants onto the ground.

"Don't sneak up on me like that Aiden! You scared me half to death!"

"How do you think I feel? I'm checking out a strange sound and your ass flies out at me."

"Sorry, I went to do my business and while I was polishing, something crawled over my foot. I hate creepy crawly things." he says, shuddering while he pulls up his pants.

"No sign of Nathaniel or my mother?" I ask.

"Sorry Aiden, no sign of them yet."

I sigh. "They are really worrying me now."

"Don't worry too much. Not many things are going to mess with an Akuma."

"Just remember she doesn't look like one right now."

"Oh yes." he sighs.

"So, they just look like a man and his pup all alone. Yes, nothing to be worried about." I say sarcastically.

"You better get some sleep Mac. I'll be up for a while."

"No, I don't see me sleeping while there are creepy crawlies around." Mac says, nervously looking around.

I laugh. "Mac, I have seen you go up against some of the scariest, nastiest things, but I never thought some creepy crawlies would get to you." I say, letting myself laugh harder.

"Creepy crawlies get into small places and I have a lot of them. That is the scariest thing of all so don't mock me," he says defensively.

"Don't be so defensive. I was only playing with you. Honestly, I woke up from something crawling up my ankle and I didn't like it one bit."

Mac looks at me quizzically.

"What's with the face Mac?"

"This face?" he says, trying to lighten the mood. "I was born with it."

"You know what I mean."

"I don't want to alarm you, but something doesn't feel right." Mac admits.

"Why do you say that? Saying I don't want to alarm you is definitely going to alarm me!"

It takes him a few moments to gather himself, "something is not right." he repeats.

"Stop going around in circles. What is going on?"

Mac has moved over to Luc, standing over his sleeping body. Lightly, he taps Luc's foot with his. "Luc, get up." he grunts. Luc continues to sleep. "LUC, GET UP!" he yells. Mac kicks Luc's foot harder this time. Panic floods Mac's face. He grasps Luc by the front of his shirt, pulling Luc's limp body to him as he slaps Luc as hard as he can across the face, but still nothing. Mac lays Luc back down.

We move around camp and find from that noise alone the Andocrits should have stirred at least.

 "Mac what is going on?"

"I think that creepy-crawly you woke up from might be what has put all of them to sleep. I do not think they will wake up any time soon. I have heard of these things, Taragors. They have long, silver bodies and more legs than any man has ever counted."
"What is the antidote?"

"There isn't one without magic."

"What about this moss I'm looking for?"

"It might be our best chance at this point. So, it looks like we can't sleep at night or we will fall prey to its venom too."

"Great and if we can't wake them soon, they will all die of starvation or dehydration."

9

A Powerful Imbalance

I don't know how much time has passed while I rock myself on the floor. I know there is truth I'm meant to find here, but there is only so much I can take. The look on Leandra's face when Mitace's fear of losing her took him over, pushing him to do such an unspeakable act in front of a room full of people, sickens me.

Tom has tried to calm me, but the scene plays over and over in my head.

"I felt her fear, Tom. She was confused. They are new to these feelings and experiences. They are like children exploring the world."

"You have to go back Bree. You wouldn't be seeing this if there wasn't a good reason, I know it."

I look up through the flames into the darkness beyond, screaming as loud as I can to the maiden. "Why are you doing this to me?! Why? WHY? WHYYY?"

The ground shakes as the maiden's voice rumbles and echoes. "All will be revealed in time."

Pain rips through me as the fire dims enough to see through the flames again. I'm still on the floor, unable to stand yet. Leandra is on the floor looking very disheveled, her blood staining the small area between her thighs while she sleeps.

The air around her is hot, heavy, and carnal. Bodies are entwined, not loving acts but the most animal, primal acts. Mitace walks toward Leandra with a drink in one hand and a small plate of fruit, cheese, and bread in the other. Hands reach out for him from the masses of naked bodies rolling around on the floor. He propels their advances away with a nudge of his foot, not giving them a second thought.

Mitace reaches Leandra's side, his cloak that covered her moments before seems to have slid off her a little, exposing her far more than Mitace is now comfortable with, he places the plate and cup down at her side to pull his cloak back up, covering her naked form once again.

Leandra stirs and flinches a little when she opens her eyes to find Mitace so close at her side. He does not say a word as he sits beside her. Gently he pushes a cushion behind her, propping Leandra up enough to have some food and drink.

Leandra winces as she gingerly moves to adjust herself, causing worry to mark Mitace's face.

"Are you alright?" he asks.

Leandra shoots him a look that makes Mitace shrink back. Leandra looks around the room at the others, fornicating and losing themselves. The grunts and groans fill the room and the heat increases.

Leandra moves in closer to Mitace when a naked man walks past and winks at her.

"Why are you not acting the same as them?" Leandra asks in confusion.

"They seem to not care who they do it with. They have tried to get me to join in, but the thought sickens me. If it is not with you.... I am sorry, I cannot take back what I did. I cannot even begin to explain how I feel or what even possessed me to do such a thing. When I look at them and where they have taken this, I realize what the wise ones were saying, it took me to a dark place too, but seeing that look on your face will haunt me until long after my light is extinguished." Mitace says mournfully.

"I am not saying I'm okay with what happened nor do I understand, but I must admit, when I looked around, the first thing I thought was, I'm glad Mitace isn't doing that."

Mitace allows himself a hopeful smile. "I swear to you I'll never let anyone touch you." he says, reaching out to her, but retracts his hand quickly when Leandra flinches at his advance.

"Leandra, I'm sure I feel for you what the underlings call love. I have been running it over and over. When you love someone, you have a ceremony with flowers and talk about how you feel. Once you do the binding ceremony, you are bonded together forever. I want you with me for all ways, an eternity, feelings like that, I can't just forget like the wise ones want me to." Mitace says in almost a whisper.

"Mitace I can't explain what I feel, but I know I can't forget either. But if this keeps going as it is, the wise ones will extinguish all of us." Leandra says, placing her hand hesitantly in his.

"Let's run away where they cannot find us."

"Where would we go?" Leandra asks, annoyed at his ridiculousness.

"I have an idea. It could be dangerous, but I can't be away from you." he confesses.

Leandra sighs. "I don't know what I feel right now I... I ugh!" she says, pounding both her fists into his chest.

Mitace is a little taken aback by her sudden attack, although it is nothing too hard. The shock is what shakes him.

"I don't know!" she repeats pounding at his chest again.

Mitace catches her fist's when she raises them again. She raises her head from his chest and opens her eyes to look at him with tears trickling down her face. Mitace leans down slowly and kisses a tear away. Leandra continues to look at him, her eyes searching for answers.

"You are angry at me." Mitace reveals to her. "You are wonderful, kind and I am a monster and now you hate me." he says, lowering his head.

Leandra sighs. "I know I should, but I do not hate you. I am upset but I do not believe I am angry at you. I know I will never be the same again. Everything in my body tells me that now. I feel tainted and way off balance. I feel lost as to how we can fix this or put things back as they were before, everything inside me tells me that is now impossible.

A woman rolls out of the steaming pile of bodies and onto Leandra's leg. When two men crawl over to retrieve her, they notice Leandra. They make their way past the woman, crawling up to Leandra.

Leandra panics. There is a fear, like nothing Mitace has experienced on her face before, even when he took her innocence from her. This is a fear that shreds him. Mitace's face changes color, going red in a terrifying way when they both move to touch her.

Before they get to her, Mitace picks them both up in a fit of rage and throws them across the cave. A few gasps are heard but most of the others are so wrapped up in their acts that they don't even notice anything else going on around them.

Mitace grabs Leandra, scooping her up into his arms and wrapping her clothes and his cloak around her. He moves toward the caves exit quickly.

Once outside the cave, Mitace places Leandra down to dress her properly behind the privacy of the vines concealing the caves entrance. Once she is dressed appropriately, they make their way outside as the ground shifts and begins to rumble and crack.

"Mitace! What is going on?" Leandra shrieks.

"I don't know but it doesn't look good. We should move fast."

Leandra barely has time to process anything, before Mitace is pulling her along through the trees. They bob and weave in and out of the trees. A crash sounds behind them, causing them to look back. Right behind them where the cliff once was is a huge hole. A crack splits the ground and travels towards them.

"Leandra, run!" Mitace screams, pulling Leandra through the trees faster. Trees fall all around them as they run. The wind picks up and whips at their faces. The trees open to a clearing and they find the viewing temple.

"How is this going to help us?" Leandra asks desperately.

"I found out while the planet is absorbing the stars and the power around it, the window to below is a door too."

"Won't that cause imbalance?"

"I don't know but I'm not waiting around to lose my light, unless you want to stay, then I'll stay with you. Your fate will be my own!" Mitace yells sincerely through the whistling howls of the wind.

They move inside. Leandra moves to the viewing window and asks. "How do we do this?"

Mitace smiles, wrapping his arms around Leandra. In a moment, he locks his mouth over Leandra's, kissing her deeply. Leandra's blue eyes grow wide at first before closing, lost in the kiss. Leandra is so lost she doesn't even notice that Mitace has thrown them both into the pool and through the window. They plummet headfirst to the vast waters below, still locked in each other's arms. Just before impact, Mitace wraps his arms around Leandra's head, breaking the kiss and shielding her with his body.

A massive splash reverberates, rocking the water below. It is not very long before people surround them under the water. Besides the pale blue color of their skin and the gills at their necks they look no different from the land dwellers. In no time they are at their side helping them breach the surface.

"What were you thinking!" someone scolds.

"You could have killed yourselves. Don't swim if you don't know how." she continues as Mitace and Leandra gasp and cough up water.

"We can't thank you enough for your kindness." Mitace says as they help them to the shore of a nearby island.

Mitace notices that a very well-built man with a surfer look about him is looking at Leandra in a way that Mitace really does not like. Her hand is in his as he helps her out of the water. His ocean blue eyes look at her with a hunger Mitace knows all too well. A loud crack sounds from above, startling the water people.

"What was that?" they squeal.

"The wise ones are angry!" they scream as another sound cracks and roars.

"What is going on?" they ask absently before they dive into the water, disappearing.

Some villagers from the island come down to the water to see what is going on. A lady Mitace recognizes as the woman who just did a binding ceremony.

"Oh my, you poor, poor things. You will catch your death of cold if you stay in those wet things. My name is Naomi, come with me." she says, ushering them away from the water and up a sand bank that leads to a small gravel path.

Small wood huts line the path until Naomi ushers them into one that looks far smaller than the others, the warmth of the fireplace greets them all once they enter, all though small it is a very warm, well-built, and loving home.

"David these people need our help."

A tall man that Mitace recognizes as her bonded comes into the room. "What happened?" he asks, concerned. "Where did you come from?"

"We fell and the water people brought us to shore. We are sorry for any inconvenience we may have caused you." Leandra says.

The man laughs. "My wife has an exceedingly big heart. If you were birds, you would already be in a soft box with a belly full of food." he laughs, making Naomi blush.

"We thank you for your kindness." Mitace says.

A crack sounds in the sky as the wind picks up, howling loudly through the eaves, startling the couple. "My stars...what is going on out there?" Naomi asks.

"We have no idea. This is all new to us." Mitace replies.

Naomi takes Leandra to a room and when they come out Leandra is in a lovely blue and white dress that hugs her waist and breasts.

"Leandra, you look lovely." Mitace admits.

Leandra blushes. "You look quite lovely too. Those clothes suit you." she says, gesturing to the brown leather pants and white cotton top David gave Mitace.

"Until this weather clears up, I cannot put these wet clothes out to dry, so I'll just hang them in front of the fire." she beams.

"So how did you get here? We have never seen you before and we all know each other on all the islands, so where did you come from?" Naomi excitedly asks.

Mitace and Leandra look at each other. "It is a long story."

10

Lost and Found (Aiden)

"This is not going to be easy. How are we going to find what we need, search for Nathaniel and my mother, and stay awake?"

"We can sleep but it will have to be in shifts." Mac says.

"We can't leave Luc out here unguarded and we need to watch each other's backs." I run my hands through my hair in frustration as I pace. "Coming out here was a mistake."

"You must have had a good reason to come out here for that moss if you left the kingdom now." Mac scolds.

"In my opinion not a good enough reason now."

"What is going on Aiden?" Mac crosses his arms, giving me that stern look that means he is not letting this go.

I sigh. I unbutton my shirt and Mac's eyebrows raise. I am waiting for him to make a smart-ass comment, but it never comes. My shirt falls, showing the burn that has moved up my shoulder and down my arm. "This is why I need the moss. When I went to get the prillum with Bree in the capium fields, I fell against a capium crystal and this happened. It was much smaller at the time, but it is growing and not going away, so this moss is my best chance at this moment in time."

Mac has no reaction. He just stares off into the trees silently.

"Do you think I made the wrong choice too?"

"Yes, I do!" he snaps at me.

I drop my head. I was afraid this would be the case, but I was still unprepared for it to still sting as much as it does.

"You didn't make the wrong choice to come, you made the wrong choice to keep this from us." Mac says a little more softly. He still isn't looking at me.

"Aiden, whether you like it or not we have all chosen to stay with you. You are a great and fair ruler and an even better friend. Each and every one of us has seen things you don't ever want to know about. We have been outcasts in our own homes. Johnathan and Aria took us in and have been a wonderful family to us, but with you and Bree, we found a real place we are all happy to call home, and your people love you just as much. We have the right to know about this kind of thing." he scolds.

"Mac I really didn't mean to upset anyone, really I didn't." I say, trying to defend my actions, but I stop myself. "You are right. Before all of you, I did not really have friends, and my family has never been the same since Bree disappeared the first time. I'm so used to my problems being my own it didn't occur to me that I would hurt my friends in doing so." I say, running my hands through my shaggy black hair.

Mac smiles. "Aiden you're a great guy. Tell us more and we can be better too, trust us as we trust you." He holds out his hand to me and we shake hands, making an unsaid vow to be more open from now on.

The light has come up and Mac and I have taken turns watching over each other so we can get a little sleep. As Mac said, these little silver bugs tried creeping in while we slept, but thankfully, we both made it through the night. Luc and the andocrits have still not woken.

"It looks like your creepy-crawly theory might be accurate for the situation at hand." I say, trying to wake Anzibar again. I rest my forehead against his massive leathery head when he does not move.

"The last thing I wanted was to be right. I can tell you that." Mac says, checking on Luc.

Slowly, I stroll over to the metal carriage and examine it again. "Mac there is something about this thing that really has me thinking, I feel like Bree would know what this is."

"You think Bree is connected to this thing?"

"Yes, I know it sounds strange but I really do."

I bend over and climb into the carriage and start looking around the space inside. I find strange parchment in a secret panel in the front of the carriage. It is some sort of strange, coded message. I do not see much else. I push and twist things that move, but nothing happens. I pull some strange levers that make Mac squeal when the seat collapses. I roar in laughter at his terrified face. Still trying to gain my composure,

I continue to push and pull things until I pull two levers, I find on the floor near my feet that make a strange sound at the back and side.

Mac gets out to investigate, relieved to have an excuse to get out of the carriage. After a moment, Mac calls for me to come and see something. I move to the side and find a small door open with writing on the inside I do not understand. That's when I notice the back of the carriage has opened up and there is another secret compartment on the carriage.

Cautiously, we both approach the back. We lift the lid and almost double over gagging. The unpleasant smell from inside is obviously coming from here. Gaining control of our stomach contents, we look inside. Both our mouths drop. Inside the secret compartment is a strange bag overgrown with red, orange, and green moss.

"Aiden isn't that what we have been looking for?"

I nod my head, not saying a word.

"Well, what are you waiting for, an invitation? What does the book say about using the moss?"

I snap out of my shock and grab Bree's book out. "It says we just boil it and drink the water for ailments, cuts, burns, and affected body parts. Grind the moss into a paste and apply to the affected area. Seems simple enough."

"Yeah, if you can stomach the smell." Mac says, pinching the bridge of his nose.

"They were not wrong about the rotten oregrin flesh smell."

"What ever happened to the sweet lillulian part?"

I pull some moss up and bring it close to my nose. "The section I just tore up has a lillulian hint so if it is ground up it will smell better."

"Oh, I hope so, or how can anyone stomach it?"

We have set up a fire and boiled the moss, separating it into a liquid for the andocrits and Luc. I use the leftover paste on myself and sure enough the lillulian smell is strong enough to stomach it.

We don't have to wait long. Luc is the first to stir, showing that the moss is working. We quickly do the same for the andocrits and I am overjoyed that Anzibar is the first to wake.

"That's my boy!" I say stroking his forehead.

Luc is grumbling as he moves to sit up while I put the paste on my arm. I scrunch my nose at the smell.

"How can something smell good and bad at the same time?" I ask out loud.

"Quit your complaining and plaster that stuff on." mac barks.

"Easy for you to say." I grumble.

Luc gets up and stretches. "Wow what time is it? Why did you let me sleep so long?" he scolds.

"Trust me, it wasn't our choice. You got bitten by a Taragor bug that put you all to sleep. We found the moss we came looking for and it was right under our noses the entire time." Mac blurts out, leaving Luc confused and lost for words.

A noise grabs our attention. "What a useless nose you have. One little puffer flower and you're a mess." a voice calls out annoyed.

"Don't you dare blame me! You are the idiot who flung it in my face! Some tracker you turned out to be." a husky voice snaps back.

I race to the trees where Nathaniel and my mother emerge. "Where in the name of all things have you been?" I ask as a parent would ask their child sneaking in after curfew.

"We would have been back ages ago if someone didn't get a stuffy nose." Nathaniel glowers at my mother. She growls back at him.

"Watch it, that big drop you found could have been your last if not for me, so don't make me regret saving you" she growls, moving toward him warningly.

"Oh, please it is so hard to be even remotely intimidated by you when you look like a bupper puppy." he says, amused. She barks a loud angry bark, making Nathaniel jump back. Reina smiles, pleased with herself.

"Okay children calm down. Let us play nice now." Mac says playfully.

"What did you find out there?" Luc asks.

"It was creepy actually. But a day north we found a cabin. It is very run down now, but it looks like someone was living out here. Inside the cabin there were a few carved bowls, some strange clothes, and items, and this." Nathaniel hands me a book.

"This looks like a journal." I open it and flip through it. As I flip each page my eyes grow wider, until I snap it shut, startling everyone.

"Aiden, What's wrong?"

"Nothing, we really need to get this to Bree as soon as we can, that's all."

"That serious?"

"That important actually. Nathaniel, you did great finding this. I would tell you what it means but I think Bree needs to know first."

"So, you can read that?"

"Yes, I believe the bond Bree and I have, gives me her ability to understand this."

"Alright then, we have two choices: spend the night, rest up, and leave first light, or we get out of here as fast as we can and never come back."

The choice is clear. No one wants to spend a second longer here than we have to. Everyone is packing up or already on their andocrits.

I lift my satchel and note it is much heavier than before. I throw it over Anzibar's back and hear a muffled groan and click. Slowly, I open the satchel and find a small grubby chittle curled up amongst my things.

"What are you doing in there?"

The chittle looks at me very frightened.

"I am not going to hurt you. What are you doing out here?" I ask gently.

The others come over to me on their andocrits.

"What is a chittle doing in a place like this?" Nathaniel asks out loud.

"Good question, he seems quite shaken up."

I move my hand towards him when I notice him flinch. He's still frightened of me. I use a little of my magic to put him at ease.

The chittle begins to pop and click little sounds in its cheeks as I pet its head.

"Would you like to come home with us? We have a lot of wonderful families of chittle in our kingdom. I think you will feel right at home." I say quietly.

The chittle pops and clicks excitedly. "YES!"

My mother comes over to me as the others join her on their andocrits.

"Firstly, did you just use your magic?" she asks.

Everyone looks at me waiting for my answer. I think for a moment before scolding them for their stupid question. I look at them, realizing what they are asking.

"Yes?" I say, more as a question than an answer.

"How? All the lands are losing magic and you are using it without a thought."

"Honestly, I did not think about it. I do not use my magic much so when I did, I did not think. This has to have something to do with Bree. Do you think she is protecting my powers somehow?"

"Could be, we can't know for sure." Mac says thoughtfully.

Something rustles on the ground, making Mac nervous.

"Whatever is going on here we can discuss it far, far away from here!"

I laugh. "Getting a bit nervous there are we?"

"None of you can tell me you like it here." he huffs.

"You said 'firstly' Mother, does that mean you had something else to ask me?"

She looks at the others. "It can wait. Let us get out of here."

"Okay, let's go home."

11

The Jealousy Within

Leandra looks worried after Mitace finishes telling Naomi and David what had happened. David is the first to say something.

"If you are from up there you are wise ones. If that is the case then we had better make you some food to eat." he says, rising from his chair.

"No, please don't treat us differently. We are from above, but we do not want to be found by the wise ones. We just want to live just like you." Mitace says, trying to ease the tension.

Naomie and David look at each other, seeming to have a conversation with their eyes.

"David, will the backroom be good enough for them?" Naomi asks.

David sighs. "It would be perfect for the two of you. Naomi can show Leandra how to do her work and I can show you how to do mine. A hand might actually be what we need right now."

Naomi and Leandra exchange an excited look as Mitace and David shake hands. Over the next couple of days Leandra picks up the household chores quickly and excitedly. She tells Mitace all about the market Naomi took her to and how they bought new material for Naomi to make some new clothes for the two of them.

Naomi races out to the fields a few weeks later when she sees David. Naomi excitedly throws herself at David. He catches her just in time.

"Not that I'm complaining but what brought this on?" he asks, kissing her.

"We are going to have a baby!"

David lifts her into the air and crushes her to him. "I'm so happy!" he says, kissing her over and over again.

Mitace is confused. "Where is the baby?" he asks.

Naomi smiles as David wraps his arms around her from behind. "The baby is growing in my womb Mitace."

"I don't understand. I have heard of this before but when they speak of having a baby there is no baby."

"Mitace a baby is like a seedling. Once it starts to form inside of a woman, the baby grows like a flower. When it is ready the woman gives birth, bringing the baby into the world."

Later that night Mitace and Leandra ask more questions about babies and where they come from. Naomi and David answer all their questions, and many more they come up with.

Over the months to come Naomi grows larger. Leandra begins to take on more of Naomi's duties so Naomi can rest more. One day Leandra goes to the water's edge to gather some shells to make a mobile for Naomi's new baby, when a voice calls out to her. Abruptly she turns to find a handsome man with hair as gold as the sun and eyes as blue as the deepest ocean.

"Hello." Leandra says.

The man inclines his head. "Hello to you." he replies seductively. "You do realize that the shells are not permitted to leave the water's edge as the sea life need them." he says, calmly resting his elbows on a rock as he taunts her.

"I'm terribly sorry. I had no idea. I saw a mobile for a baby made out of rocks and wood carvings, I only thought it would look lovely to make one with shells." she replies in a panic.

The man laughs. "I am only teasing you, although the sea life uses them, there are still many shells in the sea. I'll make you a deal. If you bring me some of those fruits, I'll find you perfect shells to use for your mobile." he says with a smile.

"Fruit? That sounds great we can meet tomorrow and I'll bring you a picnic of them!" Leandra says happily.

The following day as she promises, Leandra takes a basket of fruit to the man in the same spot she met him the day before. Leandra does not wait very long before he breaches the surface and swims over to her. He reaches beneath the water and pulls out a bag of seashells.

Leandra's eyes grow wide. "Oh my, they are beautiful! I have never seen anything this beautiful or so perfect before."

"The perks of the farier we know where to find the best trading shells. This is our main way of getting a few land things." he says with a wink.

Leandra smiles. "Farier?" she asks.

"Yes, that is what our people are called." he replies, discarding the peel and popping a lillulian in his mouth.

"So, do you have a name?"

"They call me Bryce."

"Nice to meet you, Bryce, my name is Leandra."

Bryce leans forward. "Leandra." He hums her name as if singing it in song.

"You may not remember but we have already met." he says, popping another piece of fruit into his mouth.

"We have?"

"Yes, the night you and your friend fell into our waters. We plucked you from the sea and delivered you to the land safe and sound. I wouldn't expect you to remember as it must have been a troubling ordeal for you."

"Oh, yes. I am terribly sorry. How can I forget our rescuers? Everything happened so fast, it all just became one giant blur."

"I thought as much." he chuckles, popping another lillulian into his mouth.

Leandra jumps at a sound from behind her and sees Mitace.

"Who is this?"

"Oh, Mitace, this is Bryce. He is one of the farier that saved us and he found some lovely shells for me to make a mobile for Naomi's new baby."

Mitace looks at the shells with disdain. "Come Leandra, we have been looking for you. Let us go." he says, placing a hand at her back to guide her away. Leandra tries to wave goodbye to Bryce but Mitace stops her.

"What are you doing Mitace? That was very rude." she scolds.

"Rude? He's lucky that is all I was."

"What is that supposed to mean?"

"Nothing." Mitace grumbles. "I don't want you seeing him again."

"Why?"

"Because I don't like seeing you with him!"

"Why?" she huffs again.

"Because I said so!" Mitace barks.

Leandra looks at Mitace with a clear expression of hurt on her face, but she does not say another word. Leandra strengthens her hold on the shells and briskly walks back home, leaving Mitace to chase after her.

Leandra does not speak to Mitace for the rest of the day. After a conversation with David, Mitace returns home the next day with a bunch of flowers. When he sees her, Mitace hands Leandra the bouquet?

"I'm sorry if I hurt your feelings yesterday. I don't understand why, but seeing you with him hurt me. I really didn't like it at all. It is not my intention to hurt you, in fact it is the last thing I want to do. I'm afraid someone will take you from me." he confesses.

Leandra smiles. "I am not going anywhere but you cannot stop me from speaking to people. I'll respect your feelings if you respect mine." Leandra says, taking the flowers from him.

Mitace frowns but does not say anything further.

The next morning Mitace walks in to find Naomi and Leandra eating a massive breakfast. "Oh, wow anyone would think we have two pregnant women." he laughs,

Naomi looks at Leandra with a big smile. You know that could be very possible. Now that I think about it, you have been getting bigger and you have had a little nausea lately. You can come to see the doctor with me later and we can get you checked out too."

Leandra looks shocked. "But I'm sure our people can't fall pregnant."

"Just because you never did it before it doesn't mean you never could."

After the doctor checks Naomi over and confirms her baby is healthy, the doctor pulls out a horn and places it on Leandra's stomach. He feels around her stomach for a bit and after a few pokes and prods, he confirms Leandra is also pregnant.

Naomie lets out a loud squeal of delight launching herself at a very shell-shocked Leandra, wrapping her arms around Leandra tightly.

When Leandra and Naomi return, Mitace and David are given the news that Leandra is possibly further along than Naomi. Mitace is over-joyed, swinging her around in delight.

"What do we do now that we are expecting too?"

"First, you both need to do a bonding ceremony. You will be husband and wife. It is much better to be bonded than have a child without it."

"Why do you have to be bonded?" Leandra asks.

"Here it is not approved of to have a child unbonded. People look down on that kind of thing."

"I have dreamed of being bonded to you for a long time now. I can't wait!" Mitace exclaims.

"I don't understand why, but if it must be done then I guess I'll go along with it too." Leandra says.

Overjoyed, Mitace grabs Leandra again, kissing her hard.

Over the next couple of days, everyone is busy setting up everything for Mitace and Leandra's bonding ceremony.

Leandra goes around all the islands handing out invitations Naomi made for her. When she passes her final drop by the sea, she notices Bryce waving at her. Leandra walks over to him.

"I'm sorry you can't come to the ceremony tomorrow."

"You are being bound?" he asks, a little taken back.

"Yes, I'm with child, so bonding is necessary from my understanding." she replies.

"Landers do have that as a rule. We in Aquilla don't have any such thing, we are free like the water."

"That sounds nice, to be free." Leandra says with a dreamy smile.

"Do you not feel free?"

"No, a lot has happened to me lately and none of it has really been my choice. To make a choice of my own would be very freeing to me." she says, running her fingers through the water.

"You're having a child. Didn't you have a choice in that?" he asks.

Leandra lowers her head. "I better go. It was nice seeing you again Bryce." she says, moving to leave.

"Leandra if you ever need anything, I'll be there for you. I know you are with him but I would love to be your friend." Bryce says, grabbing her hand.

She smiles and nods her head to him. "Thank you, friend." Leandra replies.

Just up from the water Leandra sees Mitace, who has a furious look on his face. "I told you how I felt about you seeing him!" he snarls.

"He is my friend, and I'm not letting you stop me from talking to a friend."

Mitace grabs at Leandra's hand angrily as the storm above cracks a loud bang. Mitace and Leandra return home quickly.

The storm has gotten worse. No rain has fallen, but the sky is cracking and rumbling in anger. David races into the house, startling Naomi and Leandra.

"The water is leaving!" he blurts out in a panic.

"What do you mean leaving?" Naomi asks.

"The farier say the water is slowly being sucked above."

"What can this mean?" Naomi asks.

"I think this might have something to do with us being here." Leandra says looking out the window. "Maybe they will stop all this if we return."

"But if we return, they will extinguish our light, and now we need to think about our baby." Mitace snaps.

"I think we might be better off leaving."

12

Jacob (Aiden)

The little chittle is happily watching everything go by as we leave the swamp far behind us. It seems this little guy has been lost in the swamp for quite some time. When we finally stop off to water the andocrits and give our aching muscles a well-deserved rest, I decide to go to the water and give the grubby chittle a wash.

Once we get near the water, he does not seem to be happy with my decision as he squirms and scratches at my hands. Once I let him go, he tries to retreat to my shoulder but falls off. I catch him and lower him to the ground so he can go if he chooses. He raises his feet, refusing to let his feet touch the ground.

"You are a funny one." I remark. "I will be here with you. I will not let anything happen to you. I promise, but if you are going to continue traveling in my satchel you will need to be clean." I warn, raising an eyebrow, daring him to challenge me.

The chittle cowers a little. His ears drop in defeat. I place him down on a nearby log to undress before he can protest my letting him go.

When he sees me removing my shirt, boots, belt, and sword, he seems far more comfortable now that he knows he is not going in alone.

Slowly, I walk into the crystal, clear water while holding him close to my chest. As we sink deeper into the water, I can feel his heartbeat rapidly increase, his growing distress evident.

I try to get him comfortable with how close he is to the water now by distracting him with conversation. Whatever happened to this little guy does not look like a pleasant story and he does not trust me enough to talk much, let alone tell me anything right now so the first thing I think of to talk about is Bree.

"You know not only do I think you will love being around chittles just like you, but you will get to meet a wonderful woman I know, who will like you and I think you will love her."

He looks at me, listening to me ramble on about Bree and everything I love about her. I especially love her ability to challenge me and even put me on my ass when she gets the better of me, which is way more than I'll ever admit to her.

It works because we are now completely in the water and he has not even realized it yet. To make it more obvious, I move around the water a little harder. After a little panic for a moment, he seemed to be visibly more relaxed. I cannot move him away from my body without him getting frightened but at least he is enjoying himself now.

"So, not as bad as you thought it would be?"

He looks at me with an awkward smile and I know it to be the case.

Once he is all clean, we get out of the water and he seems a little disappointed. I sigh and shake my head with a smile. I walk over to Anzibar's satchel to pull out a towel and dry him off.

"Nathaniel?" I call.

Nathaniel comes to me quickly. "What's wrong?"

"Nothing is wrong per say I just wanted to know if you have ever seen a chittle like this before?"

Nathaniel looks at the mostly dry ball of fluff in my hands and his eyes grow wide too.

"I have never seen a chittle with multiple colors before."

"Me either, that's why I asked." I say, equally baffled.

"Those are the most beautiful blues and purples I have ever seen on a chittle. They're colorful and all, but they're always only one color."

"I guess it goes to show anything is possible." I remark, petting the very relaxed chittle.

"I think you are going to have to name him Aiden. After this I don't see him leaving your side." Nathaniel remarks with a laugh.

"I guess I should, He is unusual so maybe something unusual." I say with a smile.

"Bree would love you, I know it, so something Bree related.

"With you everything is Bree related." Nathaniel playfully taunts.

I give him a rude gesture and continue what I was saying. "Maybe something from her world. I know just the thing! Pizza!"

Everyone crowds around us. "Wow that sounds different. What is pizza?"

"I don't know but she always says how much she misses it and curling up with one was her favorite pastime. To me it sounds like a companion she once had, what do you think?"

"Aiden that sounds lovely and so perfect." my mother coos.

"It's settled. I here by name you pizza of Negalia!"

Pizza pops and clicks, obviously delighted to be given a name and seems to love it too. I bend down and place him down for a little run, but he jumps off the ground and back in my arms. I must admit I am a little shocked he is not running around like most chittle do. Usually they cannot sit still, but Pizza seems to be quite the opposite.

"Pizza I'm not leaving you. I promise. I only thought you might like to have a run around."

He snuggles up to me for a moment, seeming to contemplate if I am telling the truth or not. It really does show he has been through something and trust is an issue. A few moments later, it seems he chooses to believe me and slowly makes his way to the ground.

Pizza walks around us but continues to stay close. I pull some food and drink out so we can all have something to eat, when I hear someone calling out above the waterfall.

We look up to find a tall man in his 60's with short white hair on his head and all over his face. Slowly, we all look at each other confused and watch him descend to where we are.

As he gets closer, I notice Bree's book in my satchel begins to glow. "What in the name of magic!"

"What is it Aiden?" Reina looks concerned.

I look over to my mother. "Don't you see the book glowing?" I whisper.

They all look at each other, then at me. "No, we don't." they whisper back, confused.

A voice comes from behind, grabbing everyone's attention. How did none of us pick up on him? Even my mother did not sniff him out until he was right on top of us.

"Who are you?"

"Jacob." he beams, bouncing on his toes.

He is a nimble old man that is for sure. "What can we do for you Jacob?" I say with my strong, deep, no nonsense tone.

"Oh, no son, it's what I can do for you. I have come to give you a message from your uncle." he says with a big smile.

"What is this message?" I ask.

"Come back to Midoria as soon as you can. A sickness is spreading through Midoria and your Aunty Aria is in a real bad way." He continues to smile as if he just told us the best news in the lands and is proud, he got to tell us.

I am increasingly growing impatient with this man. "This is important and very delicate news. Why are you out here on foot? And why is this not written?"

"Oh, no time to waste. I was in the area and a furngra told me she had a message for you and I said I would gladly give it to you." he beams.

"Thank you for delivering the message." I say, inclining my head slightly in respect.

"No time to waste. You best be off." he says chipperly bouncing on the balls of his feet.

"You're right. We will be on our way right now." I say to him.

I feel we need to be cautious with him. I do feel he is telling the truth. I make my way to Anzibar. Mother is already in the stupid box saddle I find humiliating and extremely uncomfortable.

Pizza jumps into the open satchel, obviously not willing to be left behind. I notice Bree's book again. When I pull it out and flip through the pages, I notice the books empty pages at the back are writing themselves.

13

New Beginning

"Leave?" Leandra asks.

"We can't let the wise ones find out about our baby. We need to find a way to be free of them for good." Mitace says, soothing Leandra.

"But at what cost Mitace?"

"Are you willing to put our child's life at risk to find out right now?"

"But isn't that being selfish?"

"Leandra, it is scary for all of us. The wise ones getting angry at us is something we cannot afford but you are from above, and our friends. We do not want to see you hurt either." Naomi admits to Leandra.

"I am so sorry. You are our friends, and we could have made things very hard for you. I think it might be better if we do leave." Leandra sighs, rubbing her little bump.

While Leandra is packing her things for the trip ahead Naomi is fighting with Leandra about things she might need along the way. Suddenly, a gust of wind blows all the candles out.

"Oh, no. Hang on, I'll start a fire to get them all lit again." Naomi is startled when an orb of light appears, lighting up the space better than a dozen candles. She gasps "Where did that come from?"

"I...I think I did it." Leandra stammers. "I don't know how. I desperately wanted to light the room for you and the light appeared."

"Leandra, you are a wise one too?"

"No, I am not a wise one. This can't be."

"This is the magic the wise ones wield, is it not?"

"I didn't know they had magic."

"Or maybe this is why you are kept in your world to contain this power."

"Mitace, look! I think I have magic and I think you do, too."

"What are you talking about?"

"I don't think the wise ones have been controlling the weather. I think you have been."

"What are you talking about?"

"Every time the weather has gotten really bad, you have been angry."

A loud crack thunders above the house making them all cringe. Mitace gets annoyed. "You are trying to blame this on me?" Another crack of thunder hits, rumbling the ground.

Leandra gets an idea and launches forward towards Mitace, covering his mouth with hers. Wrapping her arms around him, she kisses Mitace hard, drawing out his lust for her. Quickly, the thunder and lightning subside, and the sky begins to clear.

Shocked Naomi and David look at Mitace who is lost in his kiss with Leandra.

Leandra breaks the kiss, bringing Mitace around with her. He clears his throat when he notices the attention they have gotten.

David is the first to speak. He lifts the curtains to show Mitace out the window. "Look the storm cleared up very quickly." he says, knowingly showing Mitace who is still in denial.

"Not you too David?" he asks, looking quite wounded by David's actions toward him.

"I think Leandra is right. I think you have the same powers the wise ones do. While up there on neutral ground you have no powers, but once down here the balance is off, letting your magic run wild. If you can change the weather or produce a ball of light just from your emotions imagine the things your people could do to this land with such powers." Daniel says cautiously edging away from Mitace.

"Are you really that afraid of me David?"

"If you don't know what you can do then you could do most anything without realizing it Mitace. You can't blame me for wanting to be cautious."

"Now we know the wise ones are not after us. I think maybe we should still go to give you peace of mind."

David lowers his head shamefully. "I'm sorry Mitace. I do hope to see you again and hopefully you will know what you can do and how to control it. Until then, I don't think you should be anywhere near people."

Mitace nods his head and walks out the open door that David is holding open and the moment he is outside the rain begins to fall. Mitace looks up at the sky and laughs.

Mitace and Leandra travel far to the north west until Mitace fears for Leandra going much further while with child. They find a large clearing and build a small house from trees, sticks, and clay. Mitace has found that he can use his powers to chop a tree down with a lightning bolt and produce water when they need it. Leandra has gotten much better at summoning her light.

"I think we should start writing a book about our magic and how we learn to use it so it will help our baby if he or she ends up having powers too."

"I think that is a great idea." he says planting a kiss on her head.

Bit by bit Leandra and Mitace build their home bigger and stronger as they learn. One day Leandra is trying to get the fields ready for Mitace's return. He has gone to get some seeds so they can grow their own food. Leandra hopes to be able to use the same magic Mitace does to help make the fields for his return.

Exhausted, she falls to the ground. "I'm starting to wish I was able to travel so I could have gone with him. As I get bigger this whole pregnancy is getting harder." Leandra says to herself. "I'm so lonely it would be nice to have some company." She breathes out a sigh.

A strange sound alerts her to the presence that something is nearby. She looks through the trees and sees a deer and its fawn. The fawn is small and sweet. Leandra watches the fawn play around its mother. At that moment a small fawn with big baby eyes and three beautiful, wispy tails appears right in front of her.

"Oh, my!" she says, leaning down to the creature. Where in the name of magic did you come from? She giggles as it rubs itself against her hand. "I think I'll call you a deerling." she says.

The simple enjoyment Leandra got from having some company when she was alone brought great joy to her. When Mitace returns, he gives Leandra a book. She accepts it with great excitement.

"I know exactly what this is for!" she squeals. "The very first thing going in here is how to summon a deerling. Our child will never be alone with it and I found my magic got stronger while you were away just from keeping it around while I did other things." she beams.

"Wait, are you telling me you can do multiple things?" he asks, impressed.

Leandra smiles a big smile. "You may be able to do big things I still can't do yet, but I finally found something I can do that you can't that makes me proud." she giggles.

Mitace laughs, finding her smile and laughter contagious. "How about I show you how I do what I can do, and you put it in the book when you can do it and I'll do the same when I learn to do something you can do from the instructions. How does that sound?"

"That sounds perfect!"

Leandra and Mitace did just that, nurturing their magic and teaching each other. They keep to themselves mostly and are admirably adapted to the farming life and doing quite well. Many people have come from far and wide to trade for their crops, as they are the most luscious in the land. Many came and never left, finding nearby land, and building close by just for the convenience, and not to mention the local land was the most fertile for miles around.

Leandra and Mitace made sure to be incredibly careful not to use their magic so freely as they did not wish to cause any upset like before. But whether they knew it or not, they kept coming from far and wide. In no time at all, a small village grew up around them.

Leandra was by the water's edge when Bryce breached the surface of the water.

"Leandra? What are you doing here?"

"I live here now. What are you doing here?"

"I came to meet with a friend of mine to get some things. Word is, there are incredible crops here, so I came to get some for back home."

"How is everyone?" she asks broadly, but Bryce knows who she is really asking about.

"Everyone is doing as good as can be expected. Food has not been plentiful of late and the mood around the village has not been very warm since you left."

Leandra lowers her head. "When are you going back?" she asks.

"I don't know yet. I'll have to meet up with her and see what we need first."

"Okay. Do what you came to do. Give me a little time. If you could take a few things back for me I would be incredibly grateful."

"Of course, anything for you." he smiles.

Leandra returns later that evening and Bryce is already waiting for her. "Oh, thank you for waiting. I'm sorry if I kept you waiting long."

"Oh, not at all."

Leandra drops a massive satchel of fruits, vegetables, and rice.

"Please, it will mean a great deal to me if you could take this back with you for everyone and give it out as needed. We have far more than we need, and trade is going so well we don't really need for anything."

"The food must be good. You definitely are not as tiny as before." He sniggers.

Leandra puts her hands on her hips in a protective stance. "For your information I am with child."

Bryce looks shocked by this but recovers quickly.

"This is very gracious of you. I will do as you ask." He grabs for the satchel but hesitates. "Even with my strength and speed the water will damage all of this by the time I get there." he realizes.

Leandra smiles. "This satchel has my magic in it, making it light and watertight for safe travel back and forth. If you need more you can easily use this to help you."

"Thank you, Leandra." he says, grabbing her hand.

Leandra pulls away before his lips can touch her hand. Startled, he raises his eyebrows at the rejection.

"I am so sorry Bryce, but Mitace does not like me talking to you as it is, and I don't need him losing his temper and destroying all our hard work."

Bryce smiles. "Of course, I understand." He smiles at her one last time and sinks beneath the water, taking the loaded satchel with him.

14

Midoria Fever (Aiden)

Midoria Fever (Aiden)

"Aiden?" my mother calls to me.

"What is the hold up?" Mac asks, coming over to us.

"We are all ready to go. How about you?" Nathaniel asks, joining Mac.

Quickly, I snap the book shut and stuff it back into my satchel. I move quickly, joining mother in the dreaded box.

"Alright, ready to go so let's go!" I say moving away from the water, catching everyone off guard at my abruptness. I incline my head again to Jacob as we leave. He smiles and waves goodbye to us.

Mother curls herself around me. "Want to tell me what just happened?" she asks.

"Not really," I reply dryly.

"You have been acting strange for a while what is going on?"

"Mind your own business, Mother." I retort, my irritation getting the better of me.

"Well, you can discuss how that arm is going as I saw it is still giving you trouble, or you can tell me what was going on with that book of Bree's just now. It is a long trip to Midoria and I am very persistent when it comes to the BUSINESS of MY son." She waits a moment knowing I am realizing she will not be letting me get away with this.

I sigh. "The arm is still no better but the paste is keeping it from getting worse at the moment, so I'm considering this as a win still. The book, well it began to glow and all the back pages that were blank before are now not blank." I say in a rush hoping this will end this conversation now that I have answered her questions, but I know better.

"Why didn't you tell me about your arm sooner?!" she barks angrily.

I roll my eyes at her.

"Don't you roll your eyes at me! This is serious Aiden."

"And what could you do if you knew?" I ask, shutting her down. She knows the truth. This was my only lead and hope.

After a few moments of awkward blissful silence, she starts up again. This time asking more about the book.

"I told you everything. I snapped it closed before I really saw anything, and from what I did see, Bree needs to be the first to see it."

"And what are you going to do if that book is connected to getting her out?"

"I know it isn't!" I snap.

"What if she doesn't come back?!" she yells.

I gasp. My heart is pumping so loud, and my breath is so heavy it stings. I clench my fists, trying to rain in my growing temper.

"I'm sorry." she stutters, obviously realizing what she has said. "I... just."

"Enough. I'm tired and it will be a long trip. I don't want to talk anymore." I say, calmer than I feel.

She does not challenge me. She lays her head down and thank all who are holy she does not say another word.

When we finally reach the borders of Midoria, it does not look the same at all. What was once a breathtaking wonderland of green is now an average, dull landscape like all others. We move deeper into Midoria and it does not get any better. We reach the castle and gasp. The leaves are wilted, the gates are unmanned, and the castle looks rundown.

"What is going on here?" I ask out loud.

Luc, Mac and Nathaniel come up beside me as we enter the gates of Midoria.

"This looks like a ghost town." Mac says, looking around the empty looking town.

When we get to the stairs Anzibar lowers himself to the floor, letting my mother and I off. I grab my satchel. Pizza clicks and pops, pleased I did not forget him.

"What are you doing here?"

My eyes shoot up to the doorway, where I see Uncle Johnathan.

"Are you going senile already, old man? I taunt.

"You watch who you are calling old man!" he admonishes.

I look at him, perplexed. You sent for us. You told a furngra to tell us to come to Midoria and that a sickness has hit Midoria, and Aunty Aria is sick with it.

"As true as all of that is Aiden, I didn't send for you. I was going to, but I thought you had your own troubles especially with Bree gone."

"She isn't gone!" I snap. "I wish everyone would believe in her like I do!"

"We never said we didn't. I am truly sorry. Aria is so sick and I'm so afraid I'll lose her." his voice cracks, showing he is desperately trying to stay strong but clearly at the end of his rope.

"Where is she?" I ask calming my anger. He needs strength now and his is running out. He does not need me raging like a child. I know Bree is safe, but is his wife?

He leads us all through the castle. It looks so abandoned it is almost creepy.

"Where is everyone?" I ask.

He stops by a door and creaks it open slightly. Behind it is five trees with faces that look a lot like.... I draw in a breath.

"That is right, with all the magic leaving the lands, all Midoria are losing their ability to be alive in the magical sense."

I race up the stairs, throwing the door open to my aunt and uncles' room. There on the bed is my aunt. Slowly, I move to her side. Her head creaks as she tries to move her head to look at me.

"You're here." she rasps.

"Of course. My favorite aunt needs me."

She tries to laugh. "I'm. your... only aunt." she teases.

I try to laugh but fail. Pizza rustles in my satchel, distracting my aunt. "This is Pizza." I say, lifting him out and showing her.

Her smile broadens, causing a creaking sound to reverberate through her body. Quickly, she stops, embarrassed.

"I'm... sorry...."

"Don't you dare." I scold. "Seeing you smile was very hopeful for me and I needed it."

A slight smile returns. Pizza hops onto the bed, leaving me for the first time since we have been together. Slowly, he moves toward her.

She lifts her hand slightly to give him a pet. He plonks himself on the bed, popping and clicking his enjoyment of her affections.

"Pizza? I ...have...not...heard...that...before." she cracks and wheezes.

"Inspired by Bree." I say with a smile. "THAT'S IT!" I say, much louder than I intend, making Aunty Aria and Pizza jump.

I rummage through my satchel and pull out some moss. I race out the door, almost bumping into everyone entering the room. Ignoring their confusion and obvious questions, I race to the kitchen.

I find the biggest pot I can and boil every last bit of the moss I brought back, which was a lot. I know Bree loves keeping this stuff for rainy days like these.

The book said the moss can act as a natural magic, which means if I can keep this pumping through her like a tea, we should be able to keep her going until Bree comes home and puts things right. I think to myself.

I return to her room and everyone's attention snaps to me when I burst through the door. I plonk the tray down on the bed side table.

"Uncle, I need you to help her up." I say in an urgent tone.

He does not ask questions. He just does as I ask. I pour the large teapot I filled from the pot and fill a cup for her. Uncle Johnathan holds her up so I can put the cup to her lips so she can drink.

I see her scrunch up her nose as the aroma hits her, but she does not complain or even say a word and after a few moments, the cup is empty, and Uncle Johnathan lets her back down to rest.

"I think we should all rest for a while and see if it works." I say hopefully.

Everyone agrees, as I thought they would since we have not had much chance to rest from all the chaos going on.

I close my eyes, but it does not take long before I am being woken again. A tall man with grey eyes and ash brown hair bursts through the door.

"Aiden there is little time left. Bree needs you!"

Quickly, I jump to my feet. "Bree? Who are you? How do you know Bree?"

He does not answer me, he just runs back out the door. I chase after him, down the stairs and out to the garden. I stop dead in my tracks.

Slowly, she turns around. Her long, brown hair blows in the breeze like a vision amongst the flowers in the garden. She looks so perfect. Slowly, I move towards her. The moment she sees me, Bree runs into my arms. I kiss her sweet, full lips, wildly, while I run my fingers through her long, brown hair.

I was so afraid I would never again feel her soft skin against mine, the taste of her lips or the sweet smell of her perfume invading my senses. I even missed the way she maddens me so much I lose all sense of self. I think still locked in our kiss, desperately wanting this moment to last forever.

I think she feels the same as me, her kisses becoming wilder and messier. "Oh, Aiden!"

"Bree!"

"AIDEN!"

I open my eyes and jump. Pizza's face hovers over me. His face is a fluffy ball of joy. He licks my face again, waking me up completely.

I groan as I sit up. "Ugh, it was only a dream."

"Aiden!"

I snap my attention to my uncle at Aria's side. Quickly, I move to her side too. Within a few moments her features begin to brighten, and her limbs begin to loosen up. Uncle Johnathan wraps his arms around his wife as tears roll down his face.

"This is a moss we found in the swamp forgotten. Bree's book says it replaces magic naturally in times of need. I don't know how long it will last but it should help until Bree can get back."

Everyone looks at me for a moment, as if challenging my faith in Bree.

My uncle smiles. "If anyone can come back from the maiden it's Bree."

Mac, Luc, Nathaniel, and my mother all chime in agreement. Eventually they all begin to talk about Bree and her impossible traits. I lean on the windowsill listening, as I look out to the vast lands outside wondering what comes next.

15

The Crystal Cave

Leandra is struggling out in the fields; she is so big now she is finding it harder to move.

"It can't be long until this baby comes." Mitace says, coming up from behind, gliding his arms around her, cupping her belly in his hands.

"Any day now the doctor said." Leandra replies, nestling into his embrace.

"It is so wonderful here. Our baby will have everything he or she could ever want. I also think it is enough for you." Mitace says, kissing her gently.

"I only have a little more to do or this section will spoil." she tells him, pushing out of his embrace and continuing her harvest of the vegetables.

Mitace sighs but does not give up. He lifts her up and places her down away from the patch she was working on. "If you insist this must be done then I will do it." He gets down on his knees and continues the work Leandra was just doing.

"This does not seem fair. You have been working out at the docks and woods all day. We are supposed to share the work Mitace." Leandra grumbles.

"Exactly, share! I don't see much sharing when our baby is weighing you down and making your work ten times harder. If I can lighten your load even a little, please let me." he says to her, his eyes and tone pleading.

One look in his eyes shuts her down for any argument she could have had prepared. A loud crack startle's them both. Mitace jumps to his feet, looking round desperately.

"Mitace was that you?"

"No, it wasn't." he replies, worry etching his features.

Screams and cries sound off in the distance. Quickly, Mitace bundles Leandra up, rushing to get her to safety.

"Mitace what is going on?"

"I don't know but I am not willing to risk you getting hurt."

A group of six people race up the path to Mitace and Leandra. Mitace is on guard but knows these people.

"Mitace!" they call to him.

"You have to help us. A bunch of people in white robes are coming this way and they are blowing up buildings and setting fire to things."

"How do you expect us to help?"

"The rumors are you can both do things no one else can." one admits.

"I am sorry, but we came here for us to get away from those who treated us differently. You are on your own." Mitace says, pulling Leandra closer to his chest.

Quickly, he races back to their home, gathers a few things, and returns to Leandra who is waiting outside and keeping watch.

"We knew this day would come eventually." Leandra says with a sigh.

"They cannot have you, Leandra. I will give myself up, long before I allow them to touch you or our baby."

He gathers Leandra and moves them through the trees, weaving and changing direction. The sun is going down which means they have been traveling for at least five hours. Mitace is clearly exhausted but his desire to protect Leandra and his baby spurs him on. A rustle from the side startles them.

"Psst, over here!"

Mitace searches desperately for the voice. Slowly, he moves forward, unintentionally cracking some twigs.

"Shhhh, be quiet." the voice calls in a growling whisper.

Mitace moves Leandra against a mound when Leandra grips onto Mitace's arms as a wave of pain hits her.

"Leandra!" Mitace blurts out in a panic as another pain hits her. She sinks her teeth into Mitace's shoulder trying to muffle her screams.

"Breathe." Mitace says, trying to calm her.

Mitace moves Leandra behind the vines covering the mound to get her out of sight when he hears footsteps. Once they are behind the vines, he sees they can move freely around the cliff face while being shielded from view.

A short way up he finds an opening. Quietly, Mitace ushers Leandra through the opening, following it into the mountain.

Leandra is breathing hard now. "I don't know how much longer I can be quiet, Mitace. It hurts so bad." She leans over, grabbing onto Mitace as a contraction hits her. She bites back a scream. "I can't go much further. This pain! Something is seriously wrong!"

Footsteps snap Mitace's attention. They are not coming from where they came from, they are coming from deeper in the cave.

"Mitace, Leandra, this way."

"Jacob?" Mitace says, his shock evident.

"What are you doing here?"

"It looks like delivering a baby very soon." he says with a chuckle.

Mitace's eyes grow wide. "Is this why Leandra is in so much pain?"

"Yes, this is all very natural." he smiles.

Leandra bites down again as another contraction hits. "How is any of this natural?! And if this is the baby coming, I don't know how any-one can do this and do it again!"

"Come with me. We can talk after." he says, moving to Leandra's side.

Mitace moves his hand in front of him. "Don't you touch her!"

"I'm not going to hurt her, but she and the baby could die if we don't help her now."

"How can I trust you?"

"Mitace look in your heart. You will know what to do." he says with complete confidence.

"How could anyone do this more than once? It's madness!"

Jacob smiles. "Just you wait until your baby is in your arms. It will all become clear in that very moment."

"The water will be perfect for her. Let us move her into the lake, the waters will help with the pain."

"Water sounds great. I can't hold out much longer!"

They move Leandra to the large clear blue lake.

"Take her undergarments off her and make sure nothing is in the way."

"What? Why?"

"Because the baby is coming from down there." Mitace's confusion is evident.

"Mitace, I promise I will help you. I will not let anyone take your family away from you. Please, trust me and let me help."

Leandra screams a gut-wrenching scream that shakes Mitace. He grabs her hand and nods to Jacob. He removes her clothes from her lower half and Leandra is moved into the water. The moment her belly is under water, Leandra seems visibly relieved.

"It doesn't take all the pain, but it really does help take the pressure from my back." All of a sudden Leandra's eyes widen. "If we are in the water when this baby comes it is going to drown!" Quickly, Leandra moves to get out of the water. "Pain be damned, I'm not going through this to kill our baby!"

Jacob laughs, stopping her from leaving the water. "The baby will be fine. I promise it will not take a breath until we bring it out of the water."

At that moment, Leandra screams harder than ever before. The clear blue lake has blood all around Leandra's legs. "Oh, no! What is happening?!" she shrieks.

Jacob helps Leandra through as Mitace rubs her back and holds her hand.

"Come on, hang on a moment. I know you want to push but I need you to stop for a moment."

"That's easy for you to say!" She screams at him.

Jacob moves his hands around under the water between Leandra's legs. The blood turns a deeper shade of red with every passing moment. Mitace is visibly growing more and more terrified.

"Alright, Leandra, now! Push!"

Leandra takes a deep breath, pushing as hard as she can, screaming her pain into every push.

"I'm so tired, Mitace. I can't do this anymore." she cries.

"Yes, you can Leandra! One more push! Come on, Leandra. You are the strongest person I know. You can do this." Mitace says, encouraging her not to give up.

Leandra takes one big breath and does as she is told. She gives one last push with everything she has, and the water begins to glow. Crystals of bright colors grow from the walls and a burst of light fills the cave. Through the blinding light, the sound of a baby crying is heard.

"Congratulations! You have a beautiful little maiden." Jacob says, handing Leandra the baby.

"Oh, she is so beautiful just like her mother." Mitace beams.

"She is so tiny." Leandra remarks, a smile brightening her face.

"You did this, Leandra. You are something incredible." he says. adoringly.

"You're not disappointed she isn't a boy?" she asks.

"Not at all. A daughter just like you, is more than I could ever dream of. I couldn't be happier." he gushes. They huddle together, fawning over their new addition.

"What are you going to call her? Jacob asks.

"I don't know yet, but I think it will have to be something fit for a flower."

"Why a flower?"

"Because Naomi told us a baby was a seed that grew until it was ready to be born like a flower." Leandra reminds him.

"Alright, so we call her flower?"

"No, I don't know yet. I really want to think about it."

"Alright. Until then, I'll call you my petal." Mitace says, pressing a kiss to her little head. The baby's eyes open a little and Leandra and Mitace gasp.

16

The Fall of Sky Town
(Aiden)

Nathaniel rests his hand on my shoulder, breaking me from my thoughts. "I think we have done all we can do here. We really need to get back."

"No, we are not going back home." I say, still looking out the window, taking everyone by surprise.

"Everyone will be panicking. If they see you still have magic, we can give hope and calm people down."

"Nathaniel is right, my son. We really should get back. All we can do is give out the moss for the people here to keep them going for a while longer, but we have far more to handle back home."

I turn to face them, walking towards them. "I know you don't understand but I have to go somewhere else."

"I think that capium burn is finally getting to you. You're not think-ing straight." my mother scolds.

I move toward her, but bite back when a voice from behind me star-tles me.

"Aiden is quite right. He needs to go to Sky Town."

I turn to find Jacob is sitting in the window I was just standing at.

"How did you get in here? I was just at that window. It is a sheer drop on the other side!" I blurt out, trying to make sense of all this. "Ja-cob? What are you doing here?" I ask suspiciously.

He laughs. "So many questions and no time to answer any of them." He swings his legs out, dropping onto the floor in my aunt and uncle's room. He walks over to me and places a gentle hand on my shoulder.

"Sky Town needs you." he says with a smile. "No time to dilly, dally." He inclines his head to everyone and walks out the room.

"Wait! How did you know my aunt and uncle needed us? They never sent a message!" I yell after him as I get to the hallway. He has vanished.

"This guy is really getting on my nerves." I grumble.

"What just happened?" Uncle Jonathan asks.

"Honestly, I couldn't tell you. That guy has been in and out so much I have not got a clue of what to think of him anymore."

"Why does he want you to go to Sky Town?" he asks me.

"I think he thinks I can help them somehow, maybe. I do not know.

All I know is he led us to you saying you needed us, and you did even though you never did ask like he said you did." I sigh, running my hands through my hair.

"Do you trust him?" Aunty Aria asks me, sounding much better than before.

I think for a moment. "Yes, I think I do. There is something about him I can't explain, and before he came, I felt it too. I have to go. I'm not expecting any of you to follow me but I am going. There is no changing my mind."

Everyone looks at each other, sharing the same questioning look.

"Well, it looks like we will be going too then." Mac sighs.

I smile, delighted they trust my decision. "Mother could I ask you to stay behind and help Uncle Jonathan?"

"Mother?" he asks, confused.

She sighs. Yes, I guess I will stay." she says, lowering her head to her paws as she curls up on the floor.

"How much did we miss?" Uncle Jonathan asks.

I laugh. "A lot and I think you will have enough time with Mother to hear all the details."

He nods his head still in shock.

"Alright, let us move out. Anything happens here, come get us." I say to my mother. Her disappointment is evident that she is being left behind.

I lean down and give her a kiss to her fur covered cheek, feeling all the scales protecting her face underneath. My act takes her and everyone else by surprise. I ignore them all and leave first, not waiting for anything that could be said next.

Anzibar is saddled and loaded, ready for the journey. Pizza is hanging out of my satchel watching everything I do until I am climbing up Anzibar's tattered leather wing and on to his back.

The moment I am on, Anzibar rises, propelling us from the ground. It feels so natural being this far from the ground, yet Bree still is not a good traveler. The thought makes me smile. I lean down and pat Anzibar's neck. "I bet it feels good not having that wretched box saddle." He jostles his head in agreeance.

The others have gathered and are finally at my side. My uncle has brought my aunt down to say goodbye. She is obviously better than she was before and looking happy to be up again even if it is with a little help from my uncle. I nod to them and Mother and lead the way through the gates and on to Sky Town.

As arranged, an oregrin is waiting for us just on the outskirts of Sky Town. We leave our andocrits in a boarding house that is attached to the Ferring station. As we are boarding, light rumbling sounds come from the distance.

"Sounds like a storm but there is not a cloud in sight." Mac says.

"That there ain't no storm, the sky is falling!" an old man yells back.

Quickly, we board the Oregrin in a hurry, glad to get away from the old man's yells of the end of the world. The Oregrin takes off. Its power-ful wings whoosh as they pump, moving its great mass through the sky.

Bree called it a whale with wings when she first saw it. From what Bree told me, they swim in the sea and not in the sky in her world.

The Oregrin moves us through the sky in brilliant time but as we press on things get strange.

"Where is everything?" I ask the captain up the front.

"This is all that is left and every day we lose more." the captain replies.

I think back to the sounds from before and the old man's rants. The sky is not falling, Sky Town islands are falling! The main island of Sky Town comes into view. The entire island is surrounded by Oregrin's.

"The island is being evacuated before it loses the remaining magic that holds it up." the captain informs us.

Oregrin's come at us in a violent flood. The captain glides the Oregrin through the swarm with expert ease, impressing me slightly.

"I really don't think it will be wise to keep going." he warns us. "What are you even here for?" he asks.

"Honestly I don't know but I do know I am right where I need to be."

Something flies past my face in a flash, making me look after it to see what it was. I see an island off the side of the main island and begin to descend to the ground. Screams and cries ring out through the sky.

"There are still people on that island!" I yell.

"Yes, it is still full. The Oregrin's were sent to empty the wealthy from the main island first." the captain informs me.

"Idiots! The main island is connected to Aquila, it will not fall until it does! The outside islands are the most vulnerable!" With every word I seethe. I watch helplessly as the island full of men, women and children plummet to the ground.

My panic and fury vibrate through my body. I hear gasps as my body is engulfed by a blue light. It is Bree's light! She is connected with me. I feel our bond and I feel her power, such incredible power! In a single thought, blue light shoots from my body straight towards the plummeting island. It surrounds the island and visibly slows its descent.

"Move us toward the mainland." I bark, struggling to control the immense strain I feel from my task.

The captain nods, moving us forward without question and the island I am fighting to push to the mainland. The island is losing altitude and I am afraid I will not get it to the mainland in time.

Luc, Mac and Nathaniel have shaken their shock off and are now cheering and encouraging me on like they would an andocrit in a race.

"That's it!"

"You've got this!"

"Look the mainland! You can do this Aiden!"

Their encouraging words do help, but the strain is indescribable, and I realize this is yet another of Bree's impossible things she does all the time, making it look so easy when right now I know it could not be further from the truth.

"The mainland is right there!" Luc yells with excitement.

"But the descent is too fast now! At this rate the island is going to crash into the side of the cliff, they're not going to make it!" Nathaniel yells through the rapid wind whipping at our faces. "There only chance is if you speed up or you can lift it higher!" Nathaniel says.

"Easy for you to say!" I groan through the weighted force I am pushing. Panic surges through me. *Bree!* My heart calls out to her with everything I have. *Please, if you can hear me, I need you now! PLEASE!*

Almost instantaneously, a wave pulses from me so strong I forget to breathe. The island propels forward faster.

"That's it!" they all cheer.

"Keep it up, they are almost there!"

My body is channeling so much power, yet I do not feel the weight I did before. That is when I see her. Bree is right here with me, holding my hands. Her eyes are closed in concentration. Her power is merging with me, a breathtaking vision.

Right at that moment, the island just touches the very edge of the cliff, barely skimming across the surface. Bree's magic pushes to the front, slowing the runaway island until it comes to a complete stop a safe distance from the cliffs edge.

I fall to my knees as Bree's magic releases me and the connection to Bree is broken. My vision goes blurry as my friends in front of me begin to sway and move until it all goes dark.

17

The Birth of Magic

Tom is immediately at my side. I open my eyes and see Tom flickering. "What is going on?" I ask as the room continues to sway.

"You passed out!" Tom yells in a panic. "Are you alright? Tell me!" he demands.

I shake my head, bringing my focus back. Tom is still flickering like a bad tv show.

"Why are you flickering?" I ask him.

"I am made of pure magic, Bree, and yours just took a major hit! What happened?"

"Aiden." I whisper.

"Aiden? How can that be? For what possible reason?" Tom is getting angry, something I rarely have ever seen except the one time in my office with my old boss. That scared me, and I had hoped I would never see him like that again. Obviously, my safety is his trigger.

"Please calm down. Aiden didn't do it on purpose, he called for my help." I say, remembering the feeling I got when we connected. I saw everything he saw and I felt everything he felt. I was right there beside him. "He was in big trouble. He saved a falling island full of people from falling to their deaths. He called for me to help him control my powers, to help him save them." I say in a proud daze.

The fire around us roars brighter and hotter. "Time is running out young maiden. Push forward through the fire and learn what you must before it is too late." the maidens voice vibrates through the room.

I get up from the floor, more determined than before. I know what is going on out there right now and whatever is going on here is the key to fixing this and saving everyone. This time, with the massive drain I just had, the fire is much harder to push back, but my determination pushes me on.

Through the fire I see Leandra and Mitace looking down at their baby. "Jacob, why are her eyes Lavender? Is that normal for newborn babies?" Mitace asks.

"No, it most certainly is not." he smiles.

"Then why are her eyes that color?" Mitace asks him in a worried tone.

"She is the first of her kind very rare indeed, and I do believe those eyes will be shielded from most for what they really are, to protect her."

"What do you mean by that?" Leandra asks him.

"People without magic will see her eyes as a normal color, most likely a hazel, she is special indeed, your baby is the first baby born of power and balance with both light and dark, we can expect great things in her future." He smiles.

"I want to go back home Mitace" Leandra says not taking her eyes off her baby.

"Are you sure about this Leandra?"

"Yes, very sure. I have never felt so strong as I do now, and I am not spending my life on the run. We built a happy home and our daughter is going to know it well. Those people need us. We are powerful on our own but together we are as strong as any wise ones that could dare challenge us. I am ready to go home and protect our new family." she says peering down at her precious baby.

Knowing Leandra has a good point, and no matter if they stay or run, at some point, they will have to face them. Cautiously Mitace leads them out the cave and back home.

When their home can be seen between the trees Mitace sees their home still as they left it. Leandra and Mitace walk out into the open and down the pathway to see the damage done to the surrounding village that built up around them. Only a few homes were left from the violent onslaught of raining fireballs that torched most of the houses. It has not taken long for the people to have already started rebuilding their homes.

"Why didn't you just leave?" Mitace asks a family who is putting the final fixes on their front door.

The family of four, mother, father, and two sons, stand stunned. The father steps forward. "The lands here are better than any other and even if you won't protect us, we will stay and protect our home." he replies, wrapping an arm around his wife's shoulders.

Mitace looks at his family and understands the man's desire to protect what is his.

A few days later Mitace is out in the fields tending to the crops when some women come rushing up to him.

"Whatever is wrong to have you in such a state?" he asks the two ladies.

"Are you the one they call Mitace that has the powers of a wise one?" they ask.

"Why do you ask?"
"Please, if you are him, we need your help. Strange things are happening just outside of the village."

Mitace leaves with them and finds a young boy of around eleven crying in a large hole in the ground.

"What is going on?"
He steps towards the small boy and the wind picks up, flicking sand, twigs, and leaves in his face. Startled, Mitace looks back at the two women.

"He has powers of a wise one?"

"We don't understand. He cannot be. He was born here of simple parents."

Mitace looks back to the small boy. "Leandra showed me how to do a shielding bubble. I will have to try and keep it up to get close to the boy." Mitace moves forward.

"Come on, boy. Come out of there, my wife and I can help you."

"How can you help me? Everyone is scared of me and I don't know how or why this is happening!" the boy wails.

"I can help you. Look, I have powers too." Mitace calls the rain down around them, but not on top of them. The boy's cries calm down as he looks around him.

"You can control the water?" he sniffles.

"I can do much more than that, little one. Calm down and we can do this together."

The boy does calm down. The winds around the boy lighten to a slight breeze, then nothing. Mitace walks over to the boy and pulls him out of the large crater he had made and holds him close.

"It's okay, I have you now. We can get through this together."

As the days go by, more and more people turn up to seek guidance from Mitace and Leandra as to how to control their magic. It was not just around their home. Magic started popping up all over the lands.

People came from far and wide with different types of magic, and together, Mitace and Leandra help them all, learning new things about their capabilities too.

"I saw a lady the other day growing a tree and her magic was green and a little girl was moving rocks from one part of her father's land to the other to help them get the earth ready for planting and her magic was the color of gold. Another man in his twenties was healing a lillulian tree and his magic was green too. I really think different types of magic have been born, earth, fire, wind, and water are the main ones I have seen."

"This could be bad though!"

"These people are adjusting to this as if it was always meant to be. Do you think that maybe this was always meant to be the design of everything?"

"Honestly, I don't know. There is so much bad but there could be so much good too. We have always lived our lives with perfect balance. There is very little balance in this world right now."

"We need to help them see the path to balance."
"The wise ones have not come for us yet. I think all this magic is throwing them off somehow. Right now, we have time but eventually they will find us."

"No one here would give us in. I believe that with all my heart. Over the last few months this place has become a village, a strong, connected village. I know we can trust them." Leandra says with complete faith.

A cry rings out in the other room and Mitace places a hand on Leandra's shoulder to keep her seated, telling her without words he will get their child.

"Good morning, my little petal." he says adoringly, lifting the tiny bundle into his arms.

A loud urgent pounding at their front door makes Mitace snap his head to Leandra. She looks at him with the same concerned look on her face. Mitace quickly places his daughter into Leandra's arms and urges her into the back room. When she is away from the front door, he opens it.

"Mitace, thank the stars! Quickly, come with me. Make sure you wear something that will cover your face."

"What is this about?"

"The wise ones have called for people to find you and give you up."

"How did this come to be?"

"Most people still worship the wise ones. When faced with the growing magic spreading through the lands, they called the wise ones for answers. The wise ones are blaming everything on you and Leandra and your baby. Everyone is fighting. Some are demanding you are all given over and others are fighting to prevent it. You must come and hear the things they are saying. Quickly!" he urges.

Mitace grabs his dark grey travel cloak, throwing it around his shoulders as he runs out the door after the man.

"The child born of augra light, a most powerful child. Her birth brought magic into your lands. Where she was born is where magic must be taken back to relieve this land of this curse." a loud voice booms as Mitace approaches the clearing.

"What if this isn't a curse but a blessing?"

"You lived your lives without magic before, you can again."

"Those with magic seem to be able to control it quickly. Great beauty can be found in all of this too."

"But great destruction can come of this. The wise ones are right."

Only someone without powers would say that!"

"Those with powers can protect those without. This looks like it will be an ongoing thing for the foreseeable future. No one knows where the baby is or where it was born. I think we just need to find a way to make this work for everyone."

The crowds roar with fury as they debate the future of the lands.

"ENOUGH!" the wise one booms.

"We will find the child and sacrifice it where it was born that will put balance back to the lands."

"You're going to kill a child?"

"If the wise one thinks that is best, who are we to question?"

"That is where we have always gone wrong. We have never asked questions! I think now is the perfect time to start."

Mitace quietly moves through the trees, keeping his hood down to conceal his face.

"This is a BABY we are talking about!" a middle-aged woman retorts at the front. "How stupid can you be if you think that a bunch of wise ones afraid of a baby is not a sign? All this magic is popping up and now the wise ones don't seem so powerful anymore, their balance is them keeping all the power and they are prepared to kill a child to do it! To me, that is not someone I wish to devote my life to!"

The space erupts with agreeance and arguing in response for the woman's open opinion.

Mitace is startled by Jacob's sudden appearance right next to him. "What are you doing here?"

"Shhhh." Jacob hushes, placing a finger to his lips.

"They are saying the place my petal was born is where she will die." Mitace says in a hushed tone.
Jacob smiles.
"This is no laughing matter!"

"Shhhh." he scolds. "I am not worried at all. They will never find the cave. I have made certain of that." he declares proudly. "No one will."

"Except Leandra and I you mean?"

"No, not even you. The cave has been moved."

"How can you move a cave?" Mitace asks, unbelieving.

"The same way the cave got here the first time, or were you so wrapped up in the birth of your child you didn't even notice the very cave that disappeared in Augra was the very cave that appeared here and welcomed your child?"

Mitace thinks back to the cave and realizes this to be very true. "How did I not see this?"

"Just as I said that's how." he smiles as they watch over the debate in front of them.

"Wait, how do you know that cave was in Augra before it came here? And how did you know Leandra and I already knew that place?"

Jacob smiles. "I'm not just a handsome face I know far more than that Mitace."

Mitace starts to back away from Jacob. "You're one of them, aren't you?"

"A wise one?" he scoffs. "Do not insult me. And if I had any intention of killing your child, I would not have gone through the trouble to keep her alive."

"What do you mean?" Mitace demands. Realizing he is raising his voice. He quickly lowers it again.

"The night your daughter was born she would have died if I were not there and Leandra as well. The baby's cord wrapped around her neck, strangling her. If not for me, they would both be dead, your daughter from obvious reasons and Leandra from the blood loss."

"Who are you?"

Jacob smiles. "That doesn't matter. What matters is that the cave will never be seen by any eyes here. You have my word with that." When Mitace turns to face him, Jacob has disappeared, leaving Mitace with even more questions.

I break away from the flames. The heat is getting to me. "I can't take much more of this."

Tom is rubbing my shoulders. "You keep saying that and yet you always find a way through, you can do this."

"My eyes." I say to the floor catching my breath.

"What about them?" Tom asks me.

"What color does everyone see?" I ask hoarsely.

"I see lavender."

"And Mia?"

"Her and everyone else sees you with Hazel eyes in Mia's world."

"You knew about my eyes?"

"Only that people with magic could see them for what they really are."

This explains how I never got asked about my eyes until the day I met Aiden, in the banquet hall, but what does this mean am I related to this baby somehow?

I look at Tom and gasp. "What is going on with you?"

Tom looks at himself and sees he is flickering so badly now I can hardly tell it is him.

"Tom? What is going on?"

Tom looks at me and sighs, his form returning to that of my deerling but even that is like disappearing smoke.

"Tom!"

"I'm sorry Bree. I had hoped I would get to take you through to the very end before this would happen but I guess all of this took more power than I had hoped."

"Tom what are you talking about?! You tell me right now!" I scream at him, my fear of what comes next shaking me to my core.

"I'm sorry Bree, but the magic you used to help Aiden also came from me and once you did that you needed to keep going. You will absorb all magic until it is time to release it if you choose it right to do so."

"Tom this is stupid. Are you saying I'm willingly killing you?"

"You're absorbing me, Bree."

"That's killing you!" I yell. "How do I fix this? Please, how?"

"You can't. You will absorb everything that is your destiny. The maiden never was the one to take all magic from the lands, it was you."

Tom's voice drifts to me with his last words as he turns to mist and disappears.

"TOM!"

18

Return to the Maiden (Aiden)

Someone is calling my name over the top of loud cheers.

"Aiden."

"Aiden, wake up!"

SMACK!

My eyes shoot open when the sharp, searing pain of a large hand connecting with my cheek wakes me abruptly.

"There we go, good as new." Nathaniel grins.

"I'll remember to return the favor someday." I grumble, rubbing my face.

"No need, I am only happy to make sure you don't miss your victory.

Get up and celebrate with these people. They have been cheering your name for hours now." Nathaniel laughs.

"I have been out for hours?"

"Sure have, that's why we thought you might need further encouragement to wake up." Nathaniel laughs flexing his fingers.

"Yeah, thanks." I say dryly, still feeling the throbbing sting to my cheek.

Nathaniel turns away from me and yells. "He is awake!"

Cheers explode around me. Slowly, I move, making my way to my feet. When I finally do so, I am greeted by the sight of a sea of people surrounding us, clapping, and cheering loudly. It takes me a few moments to register what is going on.

"You saved their lives. Every man, woman, and child, has come to thank you." Luc says in awe, looking out over the crowd.

"How are there so many? It was only one island." I say in shock.

"From what they have told us, that island was housing all the other islands people that had been rescued. They were all to be evacuated after Sky Town's main island."

"That is ridiculous, Sky Town's main island is on the same connection that the maiden platform is, at least that was what I was told. Every island should have been evacuated first."

"Well as you can see, Sky Town is the only one left in the sky now, except the maiden, that is."

"What is the plan next Aiden?" Nathaniel asks, looking out over the crowd as they continue to make their way off the large island towering over us all.

"For some reason I think I am being guided back to the maiden. I think I will take it as it comes at the moment."

"That sounds a little too broad for you. I think I might have hit you a bit too hard." he teases.

I roll my eyes at him. "I can't explain it but something is guiding me. I don't know what it is, but I feel it, something will turn up showing me where to go next."

We move off the sky bus as Bree calls it and move through the hoard of people. They all greet us with such gratitude, which I find refreshing that it took an event like this to bring people together and not look at our differences whether we have fire magic, creature magic, or air magic, right now we are all just people trying to survive.

I walk through the cheering crowd and my heart grows even more. I will help Bree save every one of these people, magic or no magic, we will unite them all in peace.

"Make it known throughout all the lands, Negalia will make room for any and all who need help, no question, and for those who wish to stay but still need assistance, I'll make sure my people make rounds with supplies to help everyone through these difficult times. Together we are strong, and we will survive this and it will make us stronger for it!"

The crowd cheers a deafening sound that travels through the mass of bodies. That is when I see Jacob. Quickly, I move in and out of the crowd trying to make my way to him, but every turn I take he seems further away. I manage to find my way out of the crowd of people to a group of trees and a very overgrown path that doesn't look like it has been used in years.

Something in me tells me to just keep going. Pizza pops his head out of the satchel at my side and makes a disapproving sound.

"Come on, where is your sense of adventure?" I ask him.

Pizza's ears droop and he slides his head down in my satchel so only his eyes peer out, making me laugh. I move through the overgrown path, cutting my way through with my sword.

This is definitely not good for the blade, I think. I move forward for what feels like an hour or two when it finally opens up.

In the clearing is a nice little wooden cottage with a decent size vegetable garden out the front. I move a little closer and see the girl I recognize from before. Her rainbow eyes are a dead giveaway, but her hair is also a rainbow of colors too, unlike the blond from before.

I knew there was something strange about her. She comes out of the cottage and hands a glass and some water to a man that looks much younger than I believe him to be. I would judge him in his late 60's, although he could get away with late 40's early 50's.

I do not know why I have been led here to that woman again. As far as I'm concerned, I would like nothing more than our paths to never cross again but something keeps dragging me into her.

I know where she is now. I do not see the need to stick around any longer. I turn and leave without a sound. I have made it back to where I left everyone when Nathaniel jumps out at me. Unimpressed, I simply sidestep his disappointing attempt at getting the drop on me.

"So where did you go?" he asks, crossing his arms across his chest. My reply is interrupted when a sharp blade flies out from behind a tree, catching him completely off guard.

"Oh, boys, play nice. I think there are more important questions to be asked." the woman chirps in Nathaniel's ear as she presses the cool metal of her blade against his neck.

I put my hands up so as not to spook her. She is tall with long, dark, wavy hair and dark brown eyes. Everything from her tight black leather pants and large full breasts that are pushed up in a tight-fitting white shirt that sits off her shoulders to the knee-high boots and leather choker at her throat are all specifically tailored to seduce and trap a man. From the look of her attire, she is a man hunter that gets most of her success from her looks, I have no doubt in my mind.

"Who are you and what do you want?" I ask directly and to the point.

She smiles, running her blade across Nathaniel's throat. "Awe, not going to play first? Maybe see if you can take down widdle ol' me?"

"What do you want?" I ask, ignoring her banter, not wanting to get sucked up in her twisted games.

"Awe, you're no fun. It does not matter who I am. All I want is Logan and Metikye, where are they?" she asks, more forcefully this time.

"Logan is dead. He was thrown off the maiden platform after magic disappeared and Metikye is well protected. What do you want with them?"

"Ugh, poo, only half the reward. Oh, well. Metikye has the highest price at least, where is he?" she asks again, pressing the blade to Nathaniel's throat hard enough now that she is drawing blood.

"He is well protected in my kingdom!" I growl.

Her lack of care that I have given her the answer she asked for chills me. Quickly, I pull my blade from my hilt, throwing it in her direction. As fast as I have ever seen, she dodges my attack and vanishes in the trees.

I move to Nathaniel to make sure he is alright. Besides a bit of blood and a nice little cut that will definitely scar, he looks like he will be fine.

"Who the hell was that and how did she get the drop on you, of all people?" I ask Nathaniel in disbelief.

"I have no idea, but *wow*! I think I'm in love." he says, wiping the blood from his cut in a daze. I roll my eyes at him, smacking him at the back of the head in hopes to knock some sense in him.

"I bet anything she is a bounty hunter and our Metikye is her target. We better get back and warn everyone." I urge.

"She smelled like sweet lillulian blossoms." he says with a cheesy grin on his face obviously not hearing a word I have said.

Oh Bree, give me strength.

19

The Starlite Butterfly

"Bree, please. We have truly little time left. I know you love him, but you need to keep going before there is no more time."

My tears are still falling, and I feel like every word she says is white noise.

"I am so sick of crying and I am so sick of losing the ones I love. I am so sick of all of it!" I yell jumping to my feet. "Maiden your desire for me to know all this is doing more damage than good and I am running out of loved ones to be lost to your cause!" I scream every word dripping with disdain.

"I know you are losing faith and I know you feel like this is all for nothing but I swear to you it is all for a very good reason and you will soon know why, please push through just a little further." her words are soft and pleading, I wipe my face, I have come this far and given up so much, if I back out now it will all be for nothing, making my decision. I push through the flames to look on as I see Mitace and Leandra at a festival with their 5-month-old baby.

They both look so carefree and happy as they walk through the throng of people, stalls line the path filled with an assortment of foods, games, and gifts to buy.

Leandra stops when she sees a stall with beautiful hair accessories. "Oh, they are so beautiful!" she squeals excitedly.

Mitace's eyes run over the exotic hair pins with beautiful jewels, combs with exquisite designs and hair ties and bows, until his eyes stop on a lovely hair scarf of soft sheer material, the design is apricot with soft blue at the ends, beautiful white blossoms, and butterflies with wings of stardust. Without a second thought he is handing it to the lady behind the stall table buying it.

Without a word he moves behind Leandra and ties it in a big, beautiful bow in her hair. He turns her to face him his eyes sparkle adoringly at his wife as he runs his fingers down her face.

"You are so beautiful." he hums leaning into Leandra pressing a soft sweet kiss to her lips, when he pulls away Leandra is blushing violently from his loving gesture, the little baby swaddled in Leandra's arm sneezes waking her up, her eyes flutter open. And the two of them look down at her adoringly.

"Bless you my little petal." Mitace says running his finger across her cheek just as he did Leandra's but far softer.

"How did we get such a quiet perfect child?" Leandra asks not looking away from her baby.

"Honestly, I ask myself that every day, she is nothing like I was expecting." he laughs.

They smile and laugh so happy, a large bang sounds overhead as the sky lights up, oo's and ahhh's can be heard all around, as they all enjoy the spectacular light displays lighting up the night sky.

A sparkling light shoots into the sky but does not explode like the others it hits the ground, turning into a group of mini chittle running through the crowd of people then disappearing.

Another bang and again the light hits the ground bursting into a mass of jubes that rise and disappear, this time bangs sound off above and below as the sky is filled with sky dancers and below animals great and small roam amongst the crowd in the most spectacular display that leaves you staring in awe.

People cheer and laugh, each burst greater than the last, Boom! A sound unlike the others echoes around the space stopping the cheers, another Boom sounds a fireball shoots across the sky and rains down on the festival landing on a nearby stall of dolls and stuffed animals instantly bursting to flames. Screams sound all around as people run for their lives as more fireballs rain down.

Mitace puts his hand at Leandra's back ushering her through the panicked mass of people. Two men fighting knock into Mitace, pushing him from Leandra, the crowd push Leandra along as she calls out for Mitace.

Leandra manages to get off to the side in between two stalls so she can try to find Mitace, a burst of blue light shoots past Leandra forcing Leandra to turn and run but she collides straight into Bryce.

"Oh, I am so sorry!" she squeals in a panic.

"It is fine, no time for that now, we have to get out of here, Quick, come with me. This way." Bryce urges, grabbing Leandra's hand. They weave in and out of the crowd until they reach the water, he leads her to a small boat, urging her in.

"Quickly! I will push the boat over to the island over there. You can hide out until everything quiets down."

Leandra pulls the blankets up around her baby, ensuring she stays warm as she climbs into the boat. Bryce gets into the water, grabbing hold of the back of the boat. He pushes the boat out to the central island.

"Thank you for doing this Bryce. It means a lot."

"Don't mention it."

"No, I mean it. Things have really gotten out of balance lately and it is really hard to know who to trust, so I mean it. Thank you."

"Again, don't mention it." he replies, pushing the boat up on the sand.

"Wow, you are an amazing swimmer. You don't need magic with skills like that." she beams.

"Easy to say when you have magic."

"What is that supposed to mean? I was only saying I cannot breathe underwater or swim with such power. I could not push a boat either! You're amazing, Bryce!"

"Amazing huh? If I am so amazing, why didn't you choose me over him?" he hisses.

"What do you mean by that?"

"You know exactly what I mean."

"Bryce, stop this. You are scaring me."

"I saved your life after that idiot endangered it! I brought you to shore. I made sure you were safe! Me! Not him. All he has ever shown is his dominance and jealousy, with me you would be loved and protected all of your days."

"I don't understand what is going on. I thought you were my friend."

"Leandra, I don't want to be just your friend, I want you to love me the same way I love you."

"You love me? How can that be? You don't even know me."

"I see more than you think. They promised me if I gave them what they wanted and in return I would get what I wanted," Bryce says, stalking closer to Leandra.

Leandra's eyes grow wide. "And what would that be? You did this, didn't you?" she asks, backing away to the boat.

He rolls his eyes. "Oh please, the water is my home. You have no chance getting away from me here surrounded by water."

"Why?"

"Because I want you and I'll show you I was the choice you should have made."

"Never!"

"We will see about that."

Bryce moves to grab Leandra, but she quickly moves out of his reach. Leandra runs to get as far away from him as she can when a jet of water flies past Leandra, forcing her baby from her arms.

"What are you doing?!"

"I am truly sorry Leandra, but my people all agree we cannot take any chances with this baby and they promised me if I did, I would get you."

"Never! You cannot have her. I swear if you hurt her or take her from me there is nothing in this world that would ever make me care for you. Ever!"

The sky above opens up into a swirling portal as Bryce continues to push the jet of water to the portal above. Fury surges through Leandra, unlike anything she has ever felt before. Her magic is reaching out, engulfing her.

"Leandra!" a voice, calls to her from behind. It's Mitace. He is just coming ashore. "Leandra!"

"He has our baby!" she screams.

Mitace runs to Bryce, tackling him to the ground. The jet of water is interrupted, dropping the baby. Leandra goes to catch her when a second jet pushes past, catching the baby once again. Leandra looks over to see faces popping up all around the island, pushing their own jets of water up to propel her baby out of her reach.

Leandra forces every ounce of magic in her body to push her towards the portal. She grows in size, reaching up to her baby, being taken higher. She pushes higher and higher until she is almost in reach.

Leandra reaches up to her baby. Just as her fingertips touch the cloth of the blanket a bolt of purple light flies past Leandra's face. She looks up to see several wise ones appear in robes above her reaching out to the child.

Leandra's eyes grow wide as her baby continues to move towards them. "Please, don't do this! She is only a baby!"

They ignore her desperate pleas. The wise ones reach for the baby, victory in their grasp, but right as she reaches them a starlight butterfly appears out of nowhere. It flies through the air with a dazzling grace like nothing ever seen before and lands on the baby.

The little baby giggles at the butterfly, in a flash of bright light they both disappear.

"NO!"

Leandra's screams rock the island. Her power seethes through her. She reaches to the skies and does the unthinkable.

"For your greed and selfishness, you will all be punished!! Until she is returned to me you will all know my pain and suffering!"

Mitace yells through his pain to Leandra, but his voice cannot be heard through her seething promises of revenge.

The winds howl as she pulls all the waters of Aquila up from their deepest depths, pushing them to the skies. A massive wall of ocean whirls around her, carrying the screams of Aquila's people as they ascend. Bryce yells desperately for Leandra to forgive him as the waters take him and his people to Augra. The wise ones try to reason with her in a panic, realizing their mistake.

Leandra is too far gone now. She grows in size as she pushes Aquilla and the farier up into Augra, pushing the wise ones from their home. The wise ones continue to call to her in desperation.

"Stop this! Our people cannot be here! They will destroy the lands! Please, Leandra! Stop this! You will destroy us all!"

Unable to fight her immense power, they try everything to plead for their lives and the future of their people, but Leandra's broken heart is in such immense pain their feeble cries do very little to reach her.

Leandra looks down at Mitace. His eyes plead with her not to do whatever it is she is about to do. Her blue eyes fill with tears. Unable to bare it any longer, she turns her face away from him, still pushing Aquila through the gateway above. When the final drop is pushed up, Leandra's heart turns to stone, rapidly it spreads through her body until she becomes a massive statue dominating the large floating island, Aquila no more.

Mitace falls to his knees his world visibly shattering from the loss of his daughter and lost love.

20

Home

I pull away. My breathing is heavy and my heart is racing so hard I can feel my heartbeat throughout my whole body. I try as hard as I can to wipe the tears away but more only replace them.

"What they did to you was horrible! I don't understand, I knew... I...I... saw...I...I don't know what I just saw!" I say, trying to make sense of my thoughts.

"I knew you could do it."

"I thought all of this was to be judged to help magic, but this was all to show me how magic came to be?"

"Yes, but not only that, this is how magic came to be and how magic will be restored, if it is seen to be in the lands best interest without you losing your life."

"I DON'T UNDERSTAND!" I yell, trying to make sense out of all of this. "My life? What does my life have to do with this? Is this because of the color of my eyes? Am I related to the baby somehow?" the questions tumble from my mouth.

"Bree, you are not related to that baby, you ARE that baby."

"I don't understand. This happened hundreds of years ago. How can this be?"

"Your father was Mitace. His aging through the years was troublesome, so after a while he started staying away from view until he found he could do illusions. As his people grew in power, he had to find new ways to keep moving around so light magic users could not find him. As the years went on, light magic turned on other magic, even themselves. They believed their magic to be superior. In the end, their thirst for power destroyed them all just like the wise ones warned they would, taking their knowledge to a dark place. But when the last light magic fell, King Kintarbie, Mitace returned. He stood out into the light taking his place as Kintarbie the last king of Negalia. With no light magic users left, Mitace gave the kingdom items imbued with small amounts of his power to give the illusion light magic was still strong and alive. All magic illusion could be seen through but his own. A few years after he took over the kingdom the starlight butterfly returned you to our current time. At this point a wife and mother was desperately needed for him to keep his child and make his story match up, the child was his and he was their king. The mother who raised you, her love for you was unmeasurable. She took you in and loved you as her own from the start. Mitace told her the truth of your true origin and she even brought you to me."

"What?"

"Yes, she brought you to me and I saw you as I had remembered. My tears began to flow that day, tears of joy to see you again and tears of sorrow I could not hold you. I sang you a song every time she brought you to me."

"And she sang it to me ever since." I whisper, remembering.

"The stories about me were true in the beginning and as the originals that worked this land died, the new generation told it a little different each time, until there was very little truth to it. I stopped talking and I think he thought it was my curse, although I was heartbroken. Over the years my hope came back. Mitace stopped visiting me and I thought he had finally forgotten about me. When he remarried, I was happy and also devastated all at the same time. But when his new wife came to see me, she admitted he had never touched her, not even once. Again, I was faced with the conflicting feeling of joy and sorrow."

"After all these years you still love him?" I ask.

"I never stopped." She admits.

"After all he did to you in the beginning. How did you get over that?" I ask.

"I must admit that was not my most pleasant memory but even though it is born of great darkness, I would never trade it or change it."

Her words stun me and I am forced to really, soak them in. She was raped in front of more than forty people and yet she still feels this way. I listen intently, hanging on her every word.

"I am who I am because of those experiences. You were given to us from that. Although not ideal, I loved your father. I didn't realize it until I learned what it was, he loved me and I feel he still does. Sometimes the greatest light can be born from great darkness. In the beginning Mitace told all who asked about the maiden, that if any stood before me they would die. He knew only you could stand before me. But over the years the stories brought people offering maidens far and wide in hopes they could bring Aquilla back, but over time the stories became twisted and the truth was lost, at this point Mitace stopped coming, his hope for our return gone, but when you reappeared you awoke something inside him, I thought was long gone. He came to me and told me you had finally been returned to us and he would find a way to free me so we could finally be together, but instead I watched another woman, although kind and loving, raise you, not I. When you were taken from us again Mitace returned to me so distraught he almost stepped on my platform just to end it all, but he found strength and pushed through hoping that you would find your way home once again, and you did." The ground under me rumbles violently.

"What's going on?"

"I can't hold Aquilla any longer. Your power has grown too great now. All the lands magic is not gone Bree, it is inside you. All this time you have been the one absorbing all the magic even Tom and now me."

My eyes grow wide. "How can this be? You're telling me I've killed my sister's husband and one of my best and closest friends. I have been the one to kill and destroy all these lives and now you're saying I'm killing my mother too?!"

I fall to my knees as tears roll down my face. I seem to have this way about things in my life, once I find the truth and find something worth hanging onto, it leaves me one way or another.

"Bree there is no time for this. You must move quickly. Your bond you have with Aiden is real and very strong. No one gave that to you, and no one can take it from you. Bree, you are born into this world, the only one of her kind. You are destined for greatness and because of the size and power of your heart, you feel the weight of the world, but you are perfectly balanced. You also carry its power. Don't forget or under-estimate that Bree."

"I can't lose you! I can't lose Tom! I want it all back, please...PLEASE! Show me how to fix this!" I wail, violently crying. "All of this is because of me and I don't know how I'm doing it or even how to fix it and like normal, no answers."

"Bree rarely anything is as it seems and if our story told you anything it should be sometimes our greatest knowledge is the things, we learn for ourselves."

"I don't understand." I cry.

"You will my precious flower, I promise you, you will. Your father and I have such faith in you."

The ground shakes again, the fire vanishing, pushing the space into complete darkness.

Faintly, I hear my mother.

"Listen to your heart and it will guide you through the darkness. Your bond is stronger than you could imagine. I have one last thing to tell you my darling child...."

My eyes grow wide as her final words are a whisper.

With no time to process, I run through the darkness as fast as I can, the ground shaking more and more as the final vestiges of my mother's magic runs out.

I know everyone is counting on me but my doubts begin to take over as I fear I will fail them all, without Tom, my mum or dad I have no idea what I must do next. I trip over my own feet in the darkness, forcing my fear to take over me. The familiar feeling of the darkness seeping back in, is suffocating me.

My hands fall to the ground beneath me as I gasp and struggle for breath. With my mother's final words to me echo in my ears, I push back the darkness, regaining some strength.

Tom can't help me like last time. BECAUSE OF ME, my mother can't help me, THIS IS ALL HAPPENING BECAUSE OF ME! I have the chance to fix this, I won't let them down. Aiden and my friends are waiting for ME! The lands have faith in ME! I refuse to lose my faith. My mother said my heart will lead me through.

Strength roaring through me, my breathing becoming easier once again, I jump to my feet, my powerful desire to fix it all surging through me.

A light in the distance bursts to life, shining like a beacon. *The maiden's beacon will light the way for those lost.* She is leading me to Aiden!

I sprint as fast as my legs will carry me, my heart beating out of my chest. Running straight into the blinding light.

When the light fades and my eyes adjust, I am back on the platform and right there in front of me is Aiden. Not caring about a single thing, I run to him. He opens his arms, welcoming me into them, crushing me to him with a force that tells me not only did he miss me, but he was never letting me go ever again, and honestly, I never want him too.

"I love you so much." we both say in unison, each of us delighted. We kiss violently, never wanting this moment to end.

Cheers, yells, and wolf whistles break our spell, bringing us back. Luc, Mac, and Nathaniel are all closing in on us.

"Come on, Aiden. Do not be greedy. Let us welcome her home too." Mac says with a cheeky grin.

"Any man that greets her the way I do, is looking to live a short life." Aiden warns.

"Hahaha! No man would dare greet her the way you do, not because they are afraid of you, but because they are more afraid of Bree!" Nathaniel laughs, Mac and Luc joining in.

I roll my eyes. "You guys never change."

"Awe, Bree, if we changed, you would be disappointed. Admit it."

I laugh, my actions unintentionally verifying just that. "Hahaha! I missed you all so much!" I admit.

"We missed you too! And boy, do we have so much to catch you up on." Luc adds excitedly.

I abruptly stop laughing when Aiden grabs my arm, anger and concern etched in every feature. "What's wrong Aiden?" I stammer confused as to what has him so upset.

His looking me up and down, when I realise what has him so upset. He has only just noticed, I am covered in burns and my dress is not much more than a shadow of what I went in with.

Without a word, Aiden takes his coat off and places it on to my shoulders, when I feel a light tug at my now very singed, tattered, and dirty white dress, that only just covers me modestly. When I look down, I see the most beautiful chittle I have ever seen.

"Hello there, who are you?" I ask him gently, I can see he is very weary of people.

His ears droop for a moment and I think he will reject interacting with me. When I notice he is still holding onto my dress, I bend down so I can be eye to eye with him.

The moment I do he leaps at me. Shocked and caught off guard, I catch him, holding him close as he pops and clicks cheerfully. I stand with him still in my arms as he does not seem to want to leave me any time soon. I smile.

"So, what is his name and who does he belong to?" I ask stroking the little chittles back.

"Well, technically I found him, and he follows me around, so mine I guess, but now I'm thinking he might like you better." Aiden chuckles. "His name is Pizza." Aiden says this adoringly as he pets the chittle's head.

I cannot help myself, I burst out laughing. Aiden and everyone are looking at me confused as to what has set me off.

"Oh Aiden, I love you so much!" I laugh harder.

"You do not like it?

"Oh, no. I love it!"

"You, told me that you love curling up with pizza when you were

THE BOND WE SHARE - 167

back home. You said it was one of your favorite things to do." Aiden says defensively.

I look into his deep blue eyes. "Aiden, pizza in the other world where I grew up... well, pizza is a food."

Almost instantly the chittle leaps from my hands and back into Aiden's. All horrified eyes are on me. I laugh even harder.

"Please don't look at me like that. Pizza is a big round piece of pastry that you put veggies, meat, and cheese on, not chittle's. I promise you." I say, moving closer to the cowering chittle who is now noticeably relaxing, knowing that he is not a food. Aiden looks embarrassed.

"I am sorry. You can change it. I just thought it was different, and he is different, and I thought you would like the reference to where you were raised." he mumbles bashfully.

I move closer to Aiden planting a soft kiss to his lips. "I wouldn't change it for the world. I love it and I think it is perfect and incredibly thoughtful. This world will be much brighter with a little pizza in it." I say, as Pizza pops and clicks his approval once again. "I have a lot to tell you, too." I say, in a more serious tone bringing everyone back to the situation at hand.

"Besides what we have been holding together without you and trying to guess Luc's real name, I'm sure our news is not anywhere near as important as what you have to tell us from being inside the legendary maiden, so I think you win the first tell all." Aiden says.

I am not sure how to just tell everything I have learned for the past few months to them. It felt like only hours to me. I decide to go with quick and honest.

I take a big breath and let it all fall out, about Mitace and Leandra's story, and them being my real parents, and the confusing part where I was born three hundred years ago. I tell them all about my birth causing a reaction that spilled magic into this world giving everyone their powers, the wise ones trying to kidnap me and about Aquila betraying my parents to the wise ones.

Then I tell them about how I was thrown through time by a starlight butterfly before they could get me, making my mother furious, and making her push Aquila up to Augra, trapping them and turning herself to stone in her grief and becoming the maiden.

"The only way magic can return, is if we have our baby in the same cave I was born into, bringing permanent magic back to the lands as our bond will have the strength to make it permanent. Oh, and lastly, Lucky."

I take a deep breath, glad to get it out but looking at all their faces, it looks like I slapped them in the face with words.

"Wait, what?"

"You're over three hundred years old?" Mac asks, with a confused look on his face.

"No, I was born over three hundred years ago but I have not lived that long. Time went on while I was not here. Wow, this is getting confusing." I admit.

Aiden furrows his brows, "But I thought Kintarbie was your father."

"Yes, he is Mitace but didn't want people to know he wasn't aging, showing he was an original, so he disguised himself as Kintarbie when he fell, taking on his identity."

"This makes sense that your mother wasn't your mother."

"What do you mean by that?" I ask.

"There is talk about you not being the true daughter of Queen Kate and therefore not the true princess of Verillia."

"Well, that is true. She was chosen to pose as my mother as to not give me away."

"Then you do not know that Queen Kate was said to have a daughter that was exiled so she could raise you instead?"

My mouth drops open, my surprise evident. "No, I didn't know." I admit.

A loud *crack* sounds above distracting us momentarily.

"So, Aquila is struggling to come down?"

"Yes, something I plan to fix right now." I raise my hand with great ease, as Aquila falls, I raise a dome to protect us from the plummeting waters.

Slowly, the islands that were thought lost begin to rise with the water until Aquila is right back where it belongs. The maiden island is now no longer suspended in the air, but surrounded by a vast ocean of crystal blue water once again.

"Wow!"

"Yeah, I know." I beam.

"Wait, I still have questions."

"I thought you would." I smile.

"The starlight butterfly, you said it teleported you through time."

"Yes, that is why you don't see many of them. They flit through all of time, making them rare and they can take things with them as you now know."

"You said your mother told you, that for magic to return, we have to have our baby in the same cave you were born in?" he asks, trying to comprehend his own words.

I smile. "Yes, that's right. I was wondering when you would get there." I laugh.

"But that could take years!"

"Or months." I retort with a knowing grin.

Finally realizing my words, Aiden throws his arms around me, lifting me off my feet and twirling me around. "WE ARE HAVING A BABY!" he yells. "I love you so much." he admits pulling me to him. I look into his magnificent, deep, blue eyes, I find myself hoping our child gets his eyes. "Wait you said one last thing, what did you mean by lucky?"

I smile. "That's his real name." I say, my smile growing wider when Luc's face goes white. "Luc, it is only a name and I think Lucky is adorable."

"LUCKY?" Mac asks, his face lighting up.

"Are you kidding me? Lucky is Luc's name?"

"Oh, my stars! I cannot believe none of us ever thought of that! Bree comes along and just blurts out his name like it was nothing. That was the closest guarded secret ever!" They fall to the floor in side-splitting laughter while Luc just stands there in horror.

"Oh, my stars! The look on Luc's face says this is for real. Oh, I cannot breathe! This is the best day ever!" Nathaniel laughs.

Mac is rolling around on the floor laughing so hard I am afraid he will stop breathing.

After a few more moments, Aiden, Mac, and Nathaniel all calm down enough to approach a still very horrified and shellshocked Luc. All three place their hands on his shoulder, snapping him out of it. He lowers his head in shame.

"Don't ever lower your head like that to us. We are family, and no name will ever change that." Aiden says honestly.

Luc nods his head, a small smile trying to find its way onto his lips.

"Your name doesn't change you, and you shouldn't change it. You are who you are because of the good and the bad, and even if you think something is bad, I have learned it can lead to something that you couldn't live without and if not for the darkness you would never have found the light." I say in a ramble.

Everyone looks at me, searching for my own meaning from that. I'm sure they realize I never would have found Aiden if it wasn't for the Akuma forcing me away from my family, starting all of this in the worst way, but it led me to so much more than I could have ever dreamed.

Luc looks at me, my words sinking in and he knows his secret being free, still has not changed our view of him. This realization spreads a smile across his face.

"Lucky!" Mac says trying to keep a straight face.

"Utter that name again and I will end you!" Luc growls.

"Clearly this must be true for you to be so defensive.

"Keep going and I will put you in a box. Luc warns.

"You can't expect to hear the biggest secret ever! And not want to say anything! Come on! We know your real name now, it is cute we should use it, that is what a name is for!" Mac grins.

I roll my eyes at the both of them as they continue to argue.

"Oh, Bree! I have this for you, and your book." Aiden says handing me my book and an old journal. "I kept it safe. I have to admit, I think I would have been very lost and maybe even dead if not for that book of yours." Aiden confesses.

I hope it was not as bad as all that but from the look on his face I am sure it was far worse.

21

The Journal

With the Book in hand I move to find a shady place, that's when I notice the massive Bloom tree that dominates the platform, it is so big and beautiful, it rivals the one back home, Aiden's gaze follows my own.

"That began to grow not long after you went into the maiden, you would not believe how fast that thing popped up and grew, it wasn't until just before you came out that it went into full bloom."

I smile. "I could think of far worse things that could have taken its place." I say looking up at it. Aiden smiles back. "It looks as though I have a new place to read" I say with a laugh.

Aiden does not seem to appreciate my joke. "The one back home is far closer, far more convenient and it has far more history." He pouts.

I giggle a little as I find myself a comfortable spot under the trees immense shade, as the others join me.

I have the book in my hand. Besides being a little water damaged and smelling a little moldy, the book is in particularly good condition; I open it and begin to read.

Journal of Kate Larson.

(3 weeks 2 days) We have been here a few weeks now and nothing is as it seems.

On our way to Egypt, our car was filled with a blinding light and when we could finally see, we found ourselves in this swamp. Thanks to Mark's military experience, he managed to keep us safe for now. He built us a small cabin to protect us from what lurked out there in the fog.

When we first got here, we got out of the car and looked around. Luckily, Mark heard some people coming and hid us, not knowing what to expect. They spoke in a strange language we could not understand.

The fact that they went straight to our car and got angry, I assume because they were looking for someone in it. I believe with all my heart they brought us here, not wanting to know how or why, we stayed quiet and hid.

{5 weeks 4 days} It is getting harder to count the days now and I'm not even sure the day's work the same here. I saw magic! Real magic! We found our-selves wandering into a marketplace. The people there were like something in a dream, a lady with hair of a beautiful black danced a breath-taking dance and every time her hair shifted the fire in her hair showed.

Just as I thought her dance was the most incredible thing I had ever seen, she flung her hands out, producing a chain of fire she weaved through the air, dancing with it with such grace.

When the dance was done her fire changed from a chain to an adorable wolf of some kind. It pranced around the crowd of people collecting a currency, I believe. When she looked at us, she noticed we had nothing to give her and was exceedingly kind to offer us some food, clothes, and a bed for the night.

We have been with Tallulah and Mandel for a while now. They have been very wonderful to us. It is a little snug with Tallulah, Mandel and their two boys, Logan and Metikye, but it is amazingly comfortable.

Mark is not picking up the local language very well, but Tallulah is very patient with me. I have come extremely far since we started with pictures and can now hold a decent conversation with Tallulah at my side helping me when I mess up, like today when I tried to ask if the fruit stall owner had some fresh berries, but apparently, I asked her for her shoe in a barrel. I was horrified but they both laughed and helped me with what I should have said.

I am fluent with the language here now and Mark is getting good too. I have to admit I enjoy it much more when Mark is messing up words and not me, so many times he has had me in stitches and now I know how much my mess ups amused Tallulah, but unlike her I am far less gracious when Mark messes up, leaving him annoyed at me, until I nuzzle up to him apologizing, he always breaks, forgiving me.

I asked Tallulah today why her and Mandel left their homes. Mandel is from Sky Town and Tallulah is from Exadore. She told me they cannot go back because if they did, her and Mandel would not be allowed together.

As it is where we are now, apparently Mandel and Logan can't show their magic. It is incredibly sad and hurts my heart that they have to hide and poor Logan, he is only two. He was so excited when he used wind magic today, but it quickly went downhill from there. He was bundled up by Mandel and brought back to the little house to pack. Quickly, a massive panic erupted, and they invited us to come with them but we had to move fast.

After that Logan was scared to use his powers. He stopped talking very much and soon stopped talking altogether.

We have found a new location that is quiet, and we all helped build it up nicely. Tallulah told me people with magic are considered royal and have a duty to the lands above their hearts. If they were found they would be separated and placed in separate households. Although the living would be far greater, they would not be together.

Confused, I asked her if magic was such an issue why did she use magic so freely in the marketplace when we first met? She told me it was a risk she was willing to take to feed her family for a while, although Mandel was incredibly angry with her when he found out, but they don't seem to be able to stay mad at each other for long.

It is so strange being with Tallulah and Mandel and their two boys, it almost feels like being back home with Mia, Tom, and my grandchildren. The only thing missing is our Bree.

Mark won't let me do anything since we found out I am pregnant again. This was a massive shock since I am 49 years old. I am grateful my skincare has kept me more youthful than most but still a baby at my age is not safe any way you look at it.

We wished and prayed for so long to have another child and at the worst time right after we thought all hope was lost, our wish was granted. Our parents agreed to let Mark and I marry when they found out I was pregnant with Mia and since we fell pregnant so young and so easily, we always thought many children would be in our future. But we gave up thinking it was no longer in our cards.

Our home was raided a month ago. We have been locked in a dungeon all this time. We are all here but not together. Tallulah and Metikye are in one cell and Logan and Mandel are in another and I am here alone. Mark was taken from me a month ago and I haven't seen him since. Tallulah has tried to comfort me, but my tears are my only release I have right now. The only thing I have to be grateful for is they didn't take my journal from me.

Two weeks have passed. I was released when they realized I had no magic. I have fought to find someone to help me but I don't know where I would even start. I found myself wandering into a new kingdom. Tired, hungry, and lost, I collapsed.

A kind man found me along the road and surprisingly stopped to help me. He took me back to his palace and that's when I found out he was a king! He asked me how I came to be in his kingdom. As Tallulah and Mandel are already in the worst place they could be, I didn't think it could hurt to tell all the truth.

He was very caring and told me I could help him with an issue and in return he would help me save my friends.

True to his word, he had them set free but even he could not keep them together. Logan and Mandel were sent to Sky Town and Tallulah and Metikye were sent to Exidore. When the king asked me for his favor, I was shocked. My price was to marry him. I told him I was married and could not marry him, but his harshness of my refusal was terrifying.

I finally agreed to marry him when he promised to keep searching for Mark, and he did not want anything from me as his heart belonged to another and he knew my heart was Mark's. The marriage was only for the people to stop wanting him to be married.

Again, true to his word, he gave me my own room full of beautiful things that reminded me of home. My brush set and mirror that was once my mother's sits on my dresser. It was the only thing I had left with me. My fear that at some point I might have to trade them to survive is far from an issue now.

I found out today how truly evil people can be. I gave birth to Mark and my daughter. The moment she was born she was taken from me and as much as I begged and pleaded, they would not let me see her.

I found that the king needed much more from me than I had bargained for. My age and being pregnant was perfect to integrate his long-lost baby daughter into the kingdom without anyone asking questions. I resented this child so much I refused to see her. My pain at losing my child because of this baby made me angry and resentful.

It took me a few months before I finally agreed to see the king's daughter after he confessed Mark was safe and caring for our daughter. He told me all about his child and the maiden.

I know Leandra is the one he genuinely loves, and this poor child was ripped from them far too soon. She was finally returned, but too late for Leandra to raise her only child.

The first moment I looked into the king's daughter's hazel eyes, I knew her name. I knew I could never resent this child. I knew the precise moment Bree stole my heart all over again. I finally knew her story and where she came from, my precious lost little girl that we found in her future to come, and funnily enough, we find each other now in her past.

Kintarbie, told me about my wedding ring today and now he Is giving me lessons each day to teach me to use it, he imbued a small amount of his light magic into it so I can do some of the same things he can do, sometimes I think of how lonely things must be for him, all alone without the one he loves and no one else like him.

As the years have gone by, I have raised Bree with all the love in the world. I spend as much time as I can visiting Leandra at the Maiden platform, but I know it isn't fair, she can't hold her like I can, and it isn't easy getting the time to go all the way out to the in-between either. I know Kintarbie knows I take *her there but he never shows his disapproval and I know he loves Leandra, but he never visits himself.*

I have decided after I take Bree to Leandra for our visit tomorrow, I will take her as far away from Kintarbie as I can, the visit to the in-between will be the perfect cover, after overhearing his threats to take her to the maiden, I can't take the chance he won't do just that, she is only 10, I know sometime in the next 2 years, something happens that sends her to us in her future, I must keep her safe until then. I know he misses Leandra, but a child could not survive what is to come simply because he is growing impatient. The barriers and enchantments around the old castle tower, that straddles Nigalia and Exidor will be the perfect place to keep her safe for a short while, but it will only be a matter of time.

Today was a huge surprise. I was hurrying Bree into an Oregrin carriage when I bumped into a small girl Bree's age as we were leaving the in-between. Her golden hair was so beautiful, but it was her emerald, green eyes that stunned me.

The little girl's father called her name and as the Oregrin left the maidens docking station. I looked down into Mark's hazel eyes. We looked at each other longingly and my heart tightened in my chest, I waited so long to find him, and he turns upright when I can't go to him. I wished so desperately to run into his arms, but I couldn't stop and go back I had to get Bree to safety before it was too late. I looked into his strong arms and saw our precious little miracle he called...Madeline.

To be continued...

About the Author H.L Jones is a mother of three beautiful children and married to the love of her life for 15 years, she has an amazing family and incredible friends. By day she is a community care nurse and by night a new author who delights in writing fantasy romance with a little sizzle.

Find me on
Hljonesauthor@hotmail.com
HL Jones | Facebook
hljonesaurthor.wixsite.com/website